The glowies moved over to the next grave, still covered with dirt and dead grass, while a young man—not much decay, no glow—clawed his way out of the newly opened grave. He rubbed away the glue holding his eyelids shut and stared around, looking confused, terrified, and betrayed.

Project much? Buffy asked herself.

Spike put his hand on her shoulder, as if he knew what she was thinking. As if he knew she was reliving that moment, clawing out of her own grave. Going from unexplainable beauty and peace to . . . no one there to explain.

"That one guy who's doing the sucking? I've got to see this . . . sucker," Buffy announced, although she had a very strong suspicion of who it was. She strode forward to get away from Spike's touch, to get away from her memories of death. She pushed her way through the group of glowies. Their flesh was cool, no heat in the light coming off it.

Spike followed at her heels. But as they got closer to the dark figure, he began to whimper.

"What's with you?" Buffy asked, glancing at him.

Spike's gaze was locked on something over her shoulder. Correction: some*one*. He stared at the being in the center of the circle, eyes filled with fear.

Buffy the Vampire Slayer™

Available from POCKET BOOKS

Apocalypse Memories

Laura J. Burns and Melinda Metz

An original novel based on the hit television series
by Joss Whedon

POCKET
BOOKS

NEW YORK LONDON TORONTO SYDNEY

™ & © 2004 Twentieth Century Fox Film Corporation. All Rights Reserved.

POCKET BOOKS
An imprint of Simon & Schuster
Africa House
64–78 Kingsway
London WC2B 6AH

www.simonsays.co.uk

POCKET BOOKS and colophon are trademarks of Simon & Schuster, Inc.

Printed in Great Britain by
Cox & Wyman Ltd, Reading, Berkshire
10 9 8 7 6 5 4 3 2 1

A CIP catalogue record for this book is available from
the British Library

ISBN 0-7434-8999-3

Apocalypse Memories

CHAPTER ONE

"I thought you would have come back with a Madonna-esque accent." Xander stepped over a root pushing through the sidewalk. "You know, quasi-British, quasi-American, quasi-moronic."

Willow wanted to smile. Xander was trying so hard, scraping the bottom of his joke barrel to come up with the Madonna thing. But she couldn't quite get her lips to obey her brain and curve up.

"What's wrong, Will?" Xander asked. "Besides the fact that you were recently invisible to all your friends and almost got your skin eaten off?"

"It's just . . ." How to explain it? "It's all so Sunny-dale. Lots of memories," she answered, giving him part of the truth.

"Not all bad ones, though." Xander scanned the street. "Okay, so we're currently passing the mall where the Judge tried to start up a death spree. And almost directly below us is where we went mano-a-claw with . . . Wait. Forget that. Across the street is where we had those really good burritos that time after the movie we wanted to see was sold out. Buffy and Riley. You and Tara. Me and, well, me, because Anya was pissy about something. The fact that I wasn't making six figures directly out of high school, I'm sure. But that's not the point. The point is, good times. Y'know, when we weren't saving the world. Remember?"

Willow actually smiled as she looked over at Taco Mike's. It all came back to her in a rush—the way her nose started to run after a few bites of the toxically hot salsa, and how Tara reached over and wiped her nose for her and everybody went "aww." Or, all right, "eww," but it hadn't made her feel like a cruddy-faced five-year-old. It was just . . . sweet.

"I miss her," Willow said, speaking aloud but talking more to herself than Xander.

"Of course you do," Xander answered. "And I had to start talking about her when I wanted to cheer you up." He slapped himself on the forehead. "Smart, Harris. Very—"

Willow put her hand on his arm. "Hey, no. Don't. I think about her all the time, whether somebody mentions her or not. And you know what's weird? I keep realizing new ways I miss her."

She used both hands to brush her red hair away from her face. "Like I found out I miss her when something good happens. I wasn't expecting that. You'd think good is just good, right?"

"Uh-huh." Xander walked right under one of the blue-and-white awnings of the stinky cheese shop without jumping up to touch it. When had he stopped doing that? While she was away? Or had he stopped doing it years ago and she just hadn't noticed?

"Well, when I was with the coven and I really connected to the earth for the first time, that's when I thought maybe I'd be okay, you know?" Willow continued.

"Yeah," Xander answered. "I remember when you wrote about that in one of your letters."

"And when I wrote the letter, I was kind of happy, as close to happy as I'd been in a long time," Willow said. "Then the next morning I was eating breakfast, and I just suddenly started crying, because I realized I didn't have Tara to share my happiness with. And it would have meant more to her than anybody."

They rounded the corner and walked in silence for a moment. "Oh, here's another important stop on The Sunnydale Memory-you'd-rather-forget Tour," Xander exclaimed, his voice a little too loud. Why did guys always seem to have such trouble with quiet? She and Tara could sit together for hours without words.

"I believe it is at this very spot that Buffy found her mom making out with our own Giles after a little too much enchanted candy," Xander rushed on, adding a tour guide impression to the loud.

"Ew, yeah." Willow wrinkled her nose, trying to get with the Xander program. "Hey, how many normal days in a row do you think we've had in this town? Best ever?" she couldn't stop herself from asking, even though she knew she was being a party pooper—again.

The smile slipped off Xander's face as he considered her question. "Maybe eleven. No, 'cause there was that slimy . . ." He narrowed his brown eyes. "I'm going with eight."

"Eight." Willow felt a layer of ice form over her intestines. "So it's gonna have to happen soon."

"What?" Xander demanded. "Have you heard something? An omen? A prophesy? Something in the *Star*?"

"No. Nothing like that," Willow answered quickly. "Well, except the *Star*. I just mean odds are a situation is going to come up pretty fast where I have to use my magick." Spears of the ice began to pierce her organs now. She walked faster, hoping that would warm her.

"That's okay though, right?" Xander loped alongside her. "Buffy will get her slay on, and whatever it is, we'll help. You got all that training in England. You're good to go, right?"

"Except I'm terrified," Willow burst out. She jerked to a stop. She hadn't meant to say that. Xander, Buffy, Dawn—sooner or later they were going to need her, need her magick. It was inevitable. She didn't want them to hesitate to turn to her. And now she'd blurted out the *T* word.

Xander looked as shocked as she felt. "Terrified," he said. "I'm trying to think if I've ever heard you use the word 'terrified.'"

"I've never been this terrified," she said.

"Okay, this is serious." Xander took her elbow and led her ten feet into the Smoothie Shack. He sat her down, bought her a strawberry-banana smoothie and took the seat next to her.

Willow gripped her waxy paper cup so tightly that the gloppy pink mix oozed over the top and down the sides. "I killed someone, remember?"

"Yeah, you went all black-eyed and veiny. Not easy to forget," Xander answered, trying to meet her gaze but only making it to the bridge of her nose.

"It felt different in England. Lots of grass, lots of accents, no history. I mean, dead kings and queens and musty old buildings, but no history involving me. Being back here . . ." The ice made its way up her throat. She swallowed hard, trying to push it back down. "I feel like if I tried to magickally repair a broken fingernail I could end up—" She shook her head viciously. "I don't even want to imagine it."

Xander slapped his hands down on the little round table. "Peanuts!"

Willow's eyebrows drew together. "What?"

"That's what they do with people who are afraid of flying," Xander explained. "They have them sit on the plane on the ground and eat airplane snacks. They don't even go off the ground at first. It's part of a desensitization program. That's what you need."

"I need to eat peanuts?"

"No, see, the white-knuckle fliers eat the peanuts until they're comfortable with it. Then they work up to sitting on the plane on the tarmac. Then sitting there while it just taxis . . . you know, baby steps."

"Okay, I get it." Willow felt the tiniest bit hopeful for the first time since she'd returned from England. "I need a magick desensitization program."

"So, what's one of the first spells you ever did?" Xander asked.

A picture popped into Willow's mind—a picture of herself on the grass in front of Sunnydale High with a pencil floating in the air in front of her. "Levitation," she answered.

"Okay. So today we do a levitation spell." Xander hauled her to her feet. "Let's go get supplies."

"Wait! What about the sitting and eating peanuts part?" Willow protested.

"It's Sunnydale. Eight days, remember?" Xander pulled Willow out the door. "But you won't have to do it alone. I know I'm not part of a British coven. And I'm no Tara," he added gently. "But . . ."

Willow gave him a one-armed hug, keeping the hand holding her sloppy smoothie outstretched. "You're the best," she told him, feeling the ice in her body begin to melt.

Xander clapped his hands like a little kid. "Let's go do some magick!"

Buffy checked the Day-Glo orange watch Dawn had given her after she'd come home late one too many times. She'd been patrolling for a few hours and had already hit most of the cemeteries. Maybe she'd call it a night. There was nothing happening in the park. Well, not unless you were looking for a quick hookup, which Buffy definitely wasn't.

And she wanted to get back home to Willow. *Not that Willow needs supervision,* she thought, feeling guilty. *Just a friend.*

I'll circle by the angel fountain, then jet, she decided. The clearing with the fountain was her favorite part of the park. The smell of the eucalyptus trees nearby always felt as if it actually got down into her lungs and scrubbed them clean. And if she'd had a really brutal patrol session, she sometimes kicked off her shoes and stuck her bare little piggies in the fountain's bubbling water. The eucalyptus and the bubbles were almost as good as a fancy spa. And the statue took her breath away. This angel was no fat little cherub. He was *manly.* As long as you ignored the long dress he wore.

She pulled out her cell and hit speed dial one as she headed over. Her own voice greeted her. She wished she didn't have to listen to the message. She thought she sounded like a six-year-old girl on the machine. Her voice wasn't really so high and squeaky, was it?

"Hey, Will, you there?" Buffy said as soon as she heard the beep. "Dawn? Anybody? No? Okay. Willow, or Dawn, dinner thoughts? No food in the house, of course. So . . . menus. Still in the same kitchen drawer, Will. Probably exactly the same menus. Whoever gets home first does the dialing. And choosing. See ya."

Buffy clicked the phone off and jammed it into the pocket of her tailored leather jacket.

Baaaa.

That was a new one. She'd heard the occasional

moan, gasp, and "oh, baby" coming from the bushes, but never a *baaaa*. She wondered what you had to do to make someone bleat. Did it require a tongue piercing, or what? Buffy looked up at the angel in the center of the fountain. "Whatever it takes, they shouldn't be doing it so close to you," she told him.

Baaaa.

That really sounded animal. Buffy glanced toward the sound. Just a quick glance. She didn't want to see anything too . . . personal.

What she saw was the most darling little lamb caught in one of the thorny bushes on the far side of the clearing. She rushed over and knelt next to it. "Ooh, lambie! What are you doing out here all by yourself?" Buffy asked, slipping into cute-baby-critter talk. "You should be . . . wherever it is that lambs live. Did you escape from the petting zoo or something?"

It stared up at her, its big brown eyes begging for help. "I'll have you free in one second," she promised it, her fingers working its spongy wool away from the thorns. "Almost done. Almost got your pretty lamb self away from the stickers."

Buffy separated the lamb from the last thorn and gave its head a pat. "There you go." The lamb's lips curved up, almost as if it were smiling at her. Buffy smiled back, until she saw the row of drool-dripping fangs.

"Huh," she said. "Those are some pretty big choppers for a little lamb."

The lamb-thing's mouth opened wider. Wider.

Buffy inched away, keeping her eyes on the fangs.

With a *crack* the hinge of its jaw snapped. The top of its head flopped back, revealing a new head underneath—the head of a wolf.

The wolf locked its yellow eyes on Buffy and shook its body like a dog after a bath, flinging bits of lamb all over the grass.

"Whoa," Buffy cried, grossed out. "Now that's something you can't put on an Easter card."

She backed away another step. The wolf advanced, its silver fur standing up in a thick ridge between its shoulder blades, its tail curled low. No waggies.

"Nice wolfie. Buffy's your friend, remember," she crooned, wrapping her fingers around the thick stake in her pocket. "Buffy set you free from the nasty bush."

The wolf opened its mouth and leapt for her throat. Buffy whipped out . . . her cell phone.

Crap. She'd grabbed her cell phone. Buffy let her body go limp the second the wolf hit her. They both went down hard. The wolf snapped at her cheek, but Buffy jammed her cell phone between its jaws before they could close on her flesh.

Snap! The phone broke in two, just as Buffy brought her knee up into the wolf's stomach with all her might. A punch to the snout, and she was out from under it.

But the wolf was furious. It stalked her around the fountain, crouched so low its belly almost touched the ground. Buffy had a stake—a real one—ready, her fingers so tight around it she could feel splinters working their way into her palm.

She waited for the wolf to make another leap.

When it was in the air, she'd jam the point right in its throat or belly and that would be the end of it.

Bad plan, Buffy thought as the wolf jumped to the marble lip of the fountain, too low to give her the angle she needed. *Really bad plan.* Sweat began to trickle down her back as the wolf made another low jump— and had her on the ground again. Its teeth had missed her throat by inches and were buried deep into her right shoulder, which made the stake in her right hand almost useless.

Have to sacrifice the manicure, she decided, and she jammed the freshly painted thumbnail of her left hand into the wolf's eye. It growled in pain but didn't release her.

The wolf twisted its head back and forth, trying to rip the mouthful of her flesh free. Buffy twisted her thumb back and forth, digging deeper into the creature's eye socket. The wolf opened its jaws wide in a howl of agony.

That was her chance. She grabbed the creature's neck with both hands, her wounded shoulder on fire, and hurled the wolf over her head. Its back hit the marble edge of the fountain, and its body went limp in Buffy's grasp.

Buffy released it, then struggled to her feet and turned around to study the wolf's corpse for a moment. A thin stream of blood trickled from its mouth into the water of the fountain. "Who'd you think I was, Little Red Riding Hood?" she asked, shaking her head. "I'm the Slayer."

As she walked out of the clearing, she reached for

her cell. She had to tell whoever was ordering food no lamb curry . . . no lamb *anything*. Then she remembered the chomped-on cell. "I should be able to call that a business expense on my taxes," she mumbled.

The wolf lies still, its body cooling. Its heart no longer beats. Blood should no longer pump through its body, but that trickle of blood that dribbled into the fountain has thickened.

Now it is a stream. And now a raging river.

The clear, burbling water of the fountain has become a blood bath. Streams of blood arc over the marble angel.

A droplet falls on his face. It runs down his cheek like a tear.

A sharp crack splits the night air. It is the sound of the marble breaking open.

A fist smashes free. A fist as beautiful as the marble, as flawless.

But this fist is made of flesh.

CHAPTER TWO

Dawn stuffed a strawberry Pop-Tart in the toaster. Yeah, one bonus of having the Slayer for a sister? Pop-Tarts for dinner. Buffy hadn't been shopping for about a century. Forget about cleaning the grunge out of the toilet or spending quality time with her, not that Dawn wanted that. But with all the possible things Buffy could spend her time doing, why had she decided to go pawing through Dawn's stuff? And not just pawing, but actually pitching some of it. It was like fascism. Fascism with Pop-Tarts!

Sprong! The Pop-Tarts sprang up. Dawn grabbed one, burning her fingers. This was so wrong. She opened the fridge, pulled out the tub of Cool Whip, dunked the Pop-Tart in and took the first delicious bite.

The blend of hot and cold, runny and crunchy . . . just yum.

Dawn grabbed the other 'Tart, carried everything into the living room, and sat facing the door. She had some things to say to Buffy the Dictator, and she didn't plan on waiting one second longer to say them than she had to. How dare Buffy throw out her things? How dare she take the one childhood toy Dawn had managed to keep all her life and toss it out like trash? Tears welled up in her eyes.

No, she told herself. *I'm pissed off. Not sad. Pissed at Buffy.*

She blinked back the tears and took a deep breath. Back in control. Furious, but with an icy exterior. Satisfied, Dawn dunked her Pop-Tart in the Cool Whip again and closed her eyes. Yummy, yum, yum.

Click. Dawn's green eyes snapped open at the sound. She leapt to her feet as the front door swung open. "I can't believe what you did!" she yelled.

Buffy kicked the door shut, wincing with the motion. "What'd I do?" she asked, examining the tear in the sleeve of her leather jacket. Dawn could see blood through the rip, but she didn't care.

"You don't know what you did? That makes it so much worse." Dawn stalked to the kitchen, grabbed a bottle of peroxide—they never ran out of *that*—and a roll of paper towels, and stomped back to the living room. "You gave away my Mr. Happy!"

Dawn launched the peroxide at Buffy, following it as fast as she could with the towels. Of course, the Slayer caught them both, no problem.

"Well, if I did, it's because you're much too young to have a Mr. Happy in the first place." Buffy stripped off her jacket and doused what looked like a nasty bite on her shoulder.

"Hello, gutterface," Dawn shot back. "Mr. Happy is a stuffed animal. He's a . . . he's . . . kind of . . . part turtle and part giraffe. I've had him since I was born, practically. He lives in my closet." Except when Dawn took him out. Just once in a while. When the world felt big and scary, and Buffy was out patrolling and Dawn needed something to snuggle up to.

"Oh, god, Dawn, you haven't looked at that thing for years," Buffy said. "Some kids came around collecting things for charity, and, yes, I gave them Mr. Goofy."

"Happy," Dawn snapped. "You had no right to do that without asking me. Mom never would have." She knew playing the Mom card was low, but she didn't care. It was easier to say that than to tell Buffy how scared she got sometimes, especially when she was all alone in the big house. "And for your information, I *was* still using him. He keeps away spiders . . . and other bad things." There, that was a little of the truth.

Buffy was staring at her now with big, sad eyes. "Dawnie, you're right, I shouldn't have—"

"Don't pretend you care," Dawn snapped, not ready to give up her mad yet. That would be too easy on the absentee-Buffy. "I'm out of here. And there's nothing but Pop-Tarts for dinner!"

"But you love Pop-Tarts—"

Dawn strode to the front door and slammed her

way out before Buffy could finish. She wished there were ten doors between her and Buffy so she could slam them all.

Buffy stared at the closed front door. She couldn't believe it wasn't still vibrating from the slam of fury her sister had given it. "Guess she didn't get my message about ordering in food." Buffy picked up one of the Pop-Tarts and dunked it in the tub of Cool Whip Dawn had left on the sofa.

"Yummy," she mumbled through the first bite. Then she sighed. She had to go after her little sister, even though every bone in her body was crying for a hot bath. Buffy grabbed her purse and headed for the door.

"Dawn!" Buffy yelled as she locked the front door behind her. "Dawn!" she called again, starting down the front walk. She checked left, then right. No Dawn. Damn, that girl could move fast. Although not when it came to cleaning the gunk out of the toilet bowl.

Buffy chose left and started to run down the sidewalk, ignoring the protests from her legs.

Something cold and hard hit the top of her head. "Aah!" Buffy cried. Just what she needed. Bird poop. Except, why the hard?

She reached up gingerly, feeling for the sticky mess in her hair. She didn't really want to touch it, but better in her hand than her hair . . .

Another cold, hard minibomb struck. It slammed into her forehead, then bounced onto the sidewalk. "Ow," she said loudly, in protest.

She tilted her head up. Three more cold, hard chunks of ice slammed into her. Ouch, ouch, ouch. Bad idea. *Note to self,* she thought. *Do not point head toward sky when sky is spitting rocklike objects.* She wrapped her arms over her head and prepared to start after Dawn again.

Before she could take a step, the hail stopped. But she'd learned her lesson the hard way. She was keeping her arms over her head until she was absolutely sure she was safe. Something was strange, though. The hail wasn't smacking her in the head anymore, but it was still making noise. She heard it thumping down on the ground all around her. Buffy dropped her arms and looked up. A huge red umbrella was protecting her from the barrage. And holding the umbrella . . . Buffy blinked at the impossibly beautiful guy. Then blinked again. He was really there. Those hailstones to the noggin hadn't made her woozy. Yep, he was there, and he was gorgeous.

"Hey, Buffy," he said.

He knows me? she thought happily. Then reality set in. *Wait, he can't know me. If he knows me, I should know him. And I absolutely could not forget him.*

Starting from the top, there was that blond hair, wheat colored and thick, and a little shaggy, like he didn't care too much about it. Then moving down, the eyes, light blue, electric blue, blue you couldn't describe blue. Eyes set in a face that reminded her, hmm, a little of her favorite statue in the park, the angel.

But the angel had long flowy robes and big wings. This guy's tight, white ribbed turtleneck showed every muscle, and he had them all, even the new ones, like the It Band they were always talking about in magazines. Buffy lowered her eyes a little, trying to be discreet.

Oh, wait. Oh no. I don't think I said anything after he said "hi," Buffy realized. She dragged her eyes back up to his face and gave him a big smile, figuring that would kind of work either way. Kind of.

"So, to your house?" the guy asked.

"Yes, please," Buffy answered.

Yes, please. She was the Slayer for chrissakes. And she was acting like a bimbette who'd never heard the words "stalker" or "date rape." Here was a guy she didn't know, who happened to know her name and where she lived. And what was she doing? Trotting along with him, meek as a lamb. Er, kitten.

Buffy knew she should be on guard, ready to attack at any second. But her instincts were quiet. Actually she felt completely safe. Completely safe . . . when was the last time she'd felt that way? *Had* she felt that way even once since she'd become the Slayer?

"Who are you?" Buffy asked, realizing she'd been wrong when she thought she felt safe. She actually felt cozy. Before she left the house she'd been dreaming of soaking in a hot tub, and now she felt as if she had been, a hot tub with lots of good-smelling bubbles where the water never got cold and there were really, really, really thick white towels waiting. And the towels were warm. And there was hot cocoa. . . .

"I'm Michael," the guy answered, his voice somehow like the hot cocoa she'd just been thinking about—sweet, but not too sweet. And warm. She knew she should be freezing. It was *hailing*. But, nope.

Michael walked her up the driveway and waited for her to find her keys. Buffy wriggled her fingers around, happy to feel for her key chain for hours if it meant spending more time with this guy. Still, she lowered her eyes and stared into the depths of her purse even though she knew it meant she'd find the keys faster.

She couldn't stand to look at Michael for too long, especially his eyes. They made her *feel* too much. Could you die from being too safe and warm and cozy? She was starting to feel like a stick of melting butter inside. Melty butter, the real stuff, that smelled so good, and tasted so good, and was such a pretty color.

"I don't get this hail," she said, slipping into babble mode just to make sure he didn't leave too soon. "I was outside a half an hour ago, and not even a cloud. Summer's barely even over, for crying out loud. And it's southern California."

Please make me stop babbling like an idiot, she thought, sending the plea out to whoever was listening. She was making a fool of herself in front of the hottest guy on the planet.

"Don't worry, Buffy, it will be hot tomorrow. So hot you can work on your tan if you want to," Michael assured her. "At least until 3:04."

"How can you be so positive, Mr. Weatherman?" Buffy asked, pleased that she'd given a response that made sense. She finally looked up at him.

He was gone. And her key chain was in her hand.

• • •

Giles closed his umbrella and peered back over Buffy's front lawn, which was littered with hailstones. What in heaven's name was going on around here? He hadn't been back in California for an hour before things got weird. Hail in Sunnydale? It was barely autumn. And it was southern California!

Could the odd weather pattern have something to do with Willow's disappearance? He made a mental note to ask Buffy when it had begun as he tapped on the front door. It swung open under the gentle pressure of his hand, clearly left ajar. *Did something happen to the others?* he thought, suddenly frightened. *Buffy's just been given the gift of another life. Has it been—* He bolted inside, his wet umbrella leaving wet spatters behind him. "Buffy!" he cried.

Then he saw her. Standing in the center of the living room, her eyes wide. *She's in shock,* he thought. "Buffy," he said gently. "It's Giles. I'm here. Have you found Willow? What's happened?"

Buffy let out a long sigh. A sigh that sounded rather . . . content. "Don't you just love bubble baths?" she asked.

She was definitely in shock. Did she even know he was there? Giles snapped his fingers in front of her face. "Buffy. You must focus. Where are the others? Have you any news of Willow?" He snapped his fingers again, trying to hold down the panic that had been multiplying ever since he got on the plane to Sunnydale.

Buffy's eyelids fluttered. Then she smiled, and before Giles knew what was happening, he was wrapped in a tight hug. "Giles! It's so good to see you!" She released him. "I want to be hostess-y. Um, would you like a Pop-Tart?"

"What I'd like is for you to sit down and tell me exactly what is happening around here," Giles told her. He pointed to the sofa, and Buffy obediently sat. Giles took the seat next to her. "Do you realize when I came in you were in some sort of trance? What's the last thing you remember?"

"I was talking to Michael," Buffy answered immediately.

"Fine. Good," Giles said, relieved that her memory appeared to be intact.

"We were talking about the weather and—" Buffy bolted to her feet. "Oh, god, Dawn!"

"Dawn?" Giles repeated. *Has something happened to Dawn as well as Willow? Is that why Buffy appears—*

"She went outside and now it's hailing and she's not even wearing a jacket or anything!" Buffy continued.

Giles stared at her, trying to assess her condition. "Well, I'm sorry to hear Dawn is out in the elements without the proper outerwear," he said slowly. He took off his wire-rimmed glasses and began to clean them with his handkerchief. "But I had assumed we'd all be more concerned about Willow."

Buffy stared at him in surprise. "Willow?"

"You left me an urgent message in England saying she wasn't on the plane," he prompted her.

Buffy's eyes flew open wide and she gasped. "Is that why you're here?" she asked in a small voice. "You came all the way from London?"

"Yes, of course," he said. Didn't she know he'd be here whenever she really needed him? "What about Willow?"

"Um, she's back," Buffy said. "Or really, she was here all the time. She was on her flight and was at the airport when we went to meet her, but she was invisible to us. It was like she made her biggest fear come true—that we wouldn't want to see her. See?"

Frighteningly, he did understand. He'd begun to understand Buffy's tangled speeches long ago. "So Willow is back. And your only problem is that Dawn is out in the cold?" he asked, still disturbed by the initial state in which he'd found her.

"Yes," Buffy answered. "I mean, no! Dawn and I had a fight, and I ran out after her, and it started to hail, and then I met this guy and I forgot all about her." Buffy frowned. "I forgot all about her. And you said I was in a trance when you got here?"

"The door was ajar, and for a moment you didn't seem to realize I'd come in," Giles answered.

Buffy took a few seconds to absorb all this. Then she gave him a tense smile. "So I know it's piddly compared to a lost superpowerful witch," she said, "but do you feel like helping me figure out what kind of demon looks like something out of a Tommy Hilfiger ad and can trance a Slayer? It didn't feel like the Dracula trance. This was a melted-butter kind of trance."

"Do you think you could be a tad more scientific in your description?" Giles asked.

"I'll try," Buffy said. "But first I have to find Dawn." She headed for the door.

"Wait, Buffy," Giles called after her. "Is the melted-butter demon dangerous?"

She hesitated. "I don't think so. I mean, not immediately. All he did was walk me home. And shelter me from the hail. And find my keys."

"And put some sort of . . ." Giles had no idea what this demon had done that could reasonably be considered demonic.

"Put some sort of whammy on me," Buffy finished for him. "Yeah. But that just means I have to find Dawn right away. Otherwise he might find her and . . . make her happy too."

Giles stared at her helplessly. "Yes, I suppose we don't want that happening," he said.

"Hey, do you think when we get back you could talk to her for me?" Buffy asked. "She needs some perspective on what's important and what's not. You're great with that one. Just look in your files under nag-a-thon 211A."

Giles felt the typical Sunnydale worry settling into his bones. But Buffy didn't seem too put out by this new demon, so he wouldn't be either. "I have an alternate suggestion." He replaced his glasses. "You take Dawn in hand, and I go upstairs and attempt to avert the jet lag I feel fast approaching. When I wake up, I'll look into Sunnydale's newest demon."

"I hear an ambulance!" Willow gripped Xander's arm with both hands, almost twisting his polo shirt into a knot. "Oh, god, Xander, we killed someone. I know it."

"Willow, listen. *Listen*," Xander ordered. "The

siren is getting fainter. It's moving away from us."

Willow tried to listen, but the sound of her own heartbeat was so loud in her ears that it was hard to tell if the siren was louder or softer. She closed her eyes and concentrated. Yes, he was right. The ambulance was going away from them. She let out a long, shuddering breath and forced her fingers to release Xander.

"Better?" he asked.

She opened her eyes. "Better."

"Good." Xander shoved his hands through his dark hair. "Good. Okay. Let's not keep running around town like crazy people. There's enough of that kind of thing in Sunnydale as it is."

"We have to find out what happened to the power bolt that you knocked out the window!" Willow protested, her voice rising with every word. *Get a grip,* she ordered herself. *Don't go off on Xander. He's the best friend you have in the world. He pulled you back from the edge. He stopped you from destroying* everything.

She could never repay him for that. Not if they both lived to be a hundred.

"I agree we need to find out what happened. But the power bolt should only have had enough juice to levitate a notebook, right?" Xander asked. "'Cause that's what we were trying to do."

Willow nodded. That made sense. It totally made sense.

"So we can agree that we're not looking for a dead person," Xander continued. "We're looking for somebody who maybe got a little push. We're looking for a toe-stubbing, maybe. We might be called on to provide some Band-Aids. If it's really serious, some Bactine. It's gonna be dangerous, but we can handle it."

Willow laughed. Xander could pretty much always make her laugh. "See, this is what I was talking about before. You just witnessed me completely wig out. The tiniest bit of magick use, and I act like we started the apocalypse." She twirled her finger next to her temple in the international symbol for wacko.

"Look around. Didn't happen. We'd recognize it, all the practice we've had," Xander said. "Do you want to try another little bitty less-than-tiny spell?"

Willow's heart shuddered. "Um, I was thinking of a different kind of desensitization. Like we take a break. And tomorrow night we have a *Sabrina* marathon."

Xander thought about it. "Can I talk in the cat voice the whole time?" he asked.

"If you must," Willow agreed.

"Then I'm in."

"My fish is dead." Dawn stared down at the thin red cellophane fish lying on her palm. "Just like I could have been."

"It's not dead, it's flat," Buffy corrected her. "And you were hiding out in the garage during most of the hailstorm." She consulted the card that explained what the fish positions meant about the person holding the fish. *Yikes,* she thought. *Flat fish is not something that will get the sour off Dawn's puss.*

Buffy decided to go for distraction. "Hey, aren't you guys glad we had no food in the house?" she asked, silently eye-begging Willow to go along with her. "Otherwise no take-out Chinese with many extra packets of bad-for-you crispy noodles thanks to the charm of yours truly."

"I love these noodles," Willow agreed, ripping open another of the greasy wax packages. "I happily get zits for these noodles, I love them that much."

"I'm not falling for it," Dawn said. "I'm not a baby. You can't just, like, shake a set of car keys in front of my face so I'll forget I wanted to eat a spider. Tell me what the card says."

When Buffy hesitated, Dawn snatched the card away from her. "Great. I'm lifeless and dull." Dawn gave Buffy an accusatory stare. "Why not add 'unimportant to sisters'?"

Buffy ignored the snotty. "Oh, your hands are probably just cold," she said. "Wrap them around your tea for a minute and try again."

"Yeah, Dawnie," Willow said as she pushed all her snow peas to one side. Buffy knew she liked to save them up for a treat at the end. "Or don't. I mean, it's a fish. A fish isn't a good judge of character. At least I don't think it would be. They have little brains. They eat worms. And we eat them. Also, this particular fish—cellophane. Generally not a great predictor of anything." Willow looked nervously from Buffy to Dawn. "Okay, perhaps trying too hard."

"I want to see what the fish says about Buffy," Dawn said.

"Sure. Fine. Hit me." Buffy held out her palm and Dawn laid the cellophane fish on top. Immediately the long ends of the fish curled up and met in the middle.

Dawn checked the card. "'Passionate,'" she spat out. "I'm a dishrag and you're a firecracker who's out picking up hot guys when you're supposed to be looking for . . ." Dawn buried the rest of the sentence in an egg roll.

Buffy gritted her teeth. Why did the Chinese place have to send the damn fish tonight of all nights? What was the problem with good, old-fashioned fortune cookies? *You're the adult,* she reminded herself. *Act like it.*

"He was a demon, Dawn," Buffy said, forcing her voice to remain calm. "So, help me think. What do you think his agenda is? He obviously wanted to make contact."

"He knew your name and everything," Willow joined in. "And he knew where you lived. You think he knows you're the Slayer?"

"It'd be kind of random if he didn't, don't you think?" Buffy abandoned her chopsticks for a fork and dug into her lo mein. She was starving. "Like, of all the girls in town, he happens to pick the Slayer for . . . whatever it is he wants girls for."

"Walking them home with a nice big umbrella and making them forget about their sister," Dawn snapped. She stood up so fast she almost knocked over her chair.

"Okay, what's the what?" Willow asked when Dawn disappeared into the bathroom.

"I'm pretty sure she's still pissy because I gave away this ratty stuffed animal she had crammed in the closet. I apologized and everything. But somehow it's total proof that I don't care about her. Or maybe it's still total proof that I don't respect her privacy," Buffy explained. "Possibly it's that I don't go to the grocery store often enough and she had to eat Pop-Tarts for dinner, except she loves Pop-Tarts for dinner. But that's why I ordered Chinese just in case."

Willow nodded in agreement.

"But maybe those stupid fish ruined everything," Buffy babbled on. "I'm not completely sure. All I know is Buffy's in the doghouse—again."

"It shows what a good job you're doing," Willow told her. "She's a normal teenager. Getting all drama queen-y over minutiae."

Buffy blinked, surprised. She'd never thought of it that way. But Willow was right. Buffy could still remember the two-day-long fight she'd had with her mother over a strawberry Fruit Roll-Up. To this day she had no idea what exactly had gotten her so angry, but at the time she'd felt positive that her mother was the worst monster on the planet. And her poor mom had been baffled. Just like Buffy was now.

Buffy grinned at Willow. "What did I ever do without you?"

A tiny twinkle appeared in Willow's eyes. It was enough. Buffy had been worried that her best friend would never feel happy again after losing Tara. Maybe being back here, back home, was enough to set Willow on the track to recovery.

Buffy took a bite of her lo mein, determined to be cheerful. "Love the baby corn. Love the miniature food of all kinds. Why do you think that is?"

"I don't know. But it's not just food. It's like doll furniture. A little tiny toilet brush is adorable. A big one does nothing for me." Willow idly picked up a red fish and placed it in her palm. The cellophane crackled as the fish rolled into a ball.

"What does that mean?" Dawn asked, as she returned to the kitchen table.

Buffy checked the card. "'Timid, fearful.' See, Dawn? These paper fish are just paper fish. They don't mean anything."

"Except I kind of am," Willow admitted, staring into her teacup.

"You am what?" Buffy asked.

"Fearful."

"No way. Pretty much everything should be afraid of you," Dawn protested. "That demon Buffy just met—he'd be out of town so fast if he knew you were back."

Willow's face paled until every freckle was visible.

"Sorry," Dawn said quickly. "I meant you're scary in a good way. 'Cause you're strong."

"It's okay," Willow said, stabbing her chopsticks into her pile of snow peas and eating them mechanically.

Being strong is what Willow's afraid of. Too strong. Too powerful. She's afraid she's going to go out of control again, Buffy realized. A shiver raced through her body. Willow out of control—that was something Buffy never wanted to re-experience.

She reached over and squeezed her friend's hand, trying to infuse Willow with the trust Buffy had in her.

And trying to keep out the tiny shard of doubt that Buffy had never been able to completely force from her heart.

"You know what all of us need?" Buffy asked. "A day at Green Beach!"

"Green Beach?" Dawn looked from Buffy to Willow.

"The backyard," Willow explained.

"With glossy magazines," Buffy said. "And fruity drinks with umbrellas, and coconut suntan lo—"

"But, Buffy," Willow interrupted. "Remember—hail."

"I have it on good authority that tomorrow is going to be a gorgeous day," Buffy answered. "Hot enough to tan."

She didn't know why she felt so confident passing along Michael's forecast, but she had a feeling he was right. Absolutely, positively right.

CHAPTER THREE

"**X**ander specials for everyone." Xander sauntered into the backyard wearing baggy shorts and a huge sombrero. He carried an inflated plastic alligator under one arm and a tray of purple drinks in his free hand.

Willow couldn't figure out if he was trying way too hard or just being Xander. This was more a pre-Anya or at least pre-breakup-with-Anya Xander, she decided. He was forcing the fun a little bit.

Giles didn't seem to be forcing anything. He sat under the biggest tree in the yard, coated with the highest SPF sunblock he could find and wearing a long-sleeved shirt and pants, his shoes and socks in place. He'd refused all of Buffy's magazines—even *Maxim*.

He had Willow's laptop on his knees as he worked on identifying Buffy's demon.

What kind of demon comes waltzing right up to the Slayer? Willow thought. *It must be extremely powerful to be willing to approach her like that.* And if it could put Buffy in its thrall, what could it do to a regular person? Was there any kind of magick that could fight it?

Giles is doing the research thing, Willow reminded herself. *Your job is to smile and make with the fake fun. At least for now.* "Okay, are you guys ready for this quiz?" Willow grabbed one of Xander's frozen Berry-Berry Quite Contrary drinks off his tray. Dawn reached for one too.

"Yours is the one with the yellow umbrella," Xander told her, catching her wrist and handing her the drink.

"Why can't—"

"Dawn, don't start," Buffy ordered.

Dawn scowled and took a big gulp of the drink Xander had given her. *Maybe Dawn should do a little pretending to have fun too,* Willow thought. *Maybe pretending is what makes the world go round.* It was a depressing thought. She decided to distract herself by plowing ahead with the fun-making.

"First question," Willow said. "Guys: boxers, tighty whities, banana slings, or commando?" She looked at Xander. He was faking being offended.

"Oh, come on, we'll answer all the girlie questions," Willow said.

"TWs, unless I haven't had time to do my laundry," Xander answered promptly. "Then I've been known to show a little cheek cleavage."

"Oh, good lord," Giles sputtered, turning as red as if he'd been baking in the sun for hours.

Willow laughed, along with Buffy and Dawn—a real laugh that ended abruptly when she felt a prickle run up her spinal cord.

"What, Will?" Buffy asked.

Willow shook her head. "Nothing." But it wasn't nothing. It was the feeling she got when something was going to happen, something not good. "Giles, you have to answer."

"I certainly do not," he said. But he took a sip of his drink and smiled fondly at them. Then he returned his attention to the laptop.

"I have a question. Say you're a woman, which all of you are except Giles," Xander began. "Say you're one of those hard-but-soft, late-twenties-early-thirties businesswomen—you know, with the toes and the nails and the hair. What kind of underwear do they want a man to wear?"

"Wait. I want to get this straight," Buffy said. "You're saying you'll become who they want? Betray your inner self to make yourself acceptable?"

"I think he's saying he'll change his underwear," Willow told her.

"Damn straight," Xander agreed.

The prickle ran up Willow's spinal cord again, but this time it didn't stop at her neck. It ran all the way up to the top of her head, and then the electric prickles began to burrow into her brain. Something was going to happen. She could feel it. Couldn't they feel it?

She looked at her friends' smiling faces. Maybe

they weren't as happy as they were pretending to be. But it was clear no one else felt something dark rushing toward them.

"Giles, are you finding anything?" she asked.

He shook his head. "Sadly, searching for handsome creatures who make one feel warm inside has led mainly to pornography sites."

Relax, Willow told herself. *You're just freaking out because you're back in Sunnydale. Relax.*

She focused on all the goodness around her: the cool dewdrops on her glass, the warm sun on her face, the smell of her cocoa butter sunscreen, the crunchy grass under her bare toes . . .

Wait. *Crunchy* grass?

Willow looked down at her feet and gave a choked cry.

"What?" Xander demanded. Then he saw it. They all saw it. The green grass of Buffy's lawn was turning brown in a rushing wave. The wave of death hit the oak tree in the corner of the backyard and the leaves went from living to dying in an instant.

Over the wooden fence Willow could see the leaves of other trees wither. As she watched, a pine tree shuddered and fell. The badness she'd felt coming had arrived.

"Giles?" Buffy said helplessly.

Willow turned toward Buffy and saw that her friend's hands were curled into fists. But there was nothing she could turn her Slayer strength against. Xander and Dawn stared wordlessly at the destruction.

"I think we need to see a little more of this and

make an assessment," Giles said. He led the way out the back gate.

"Sweet Jesus on a motorcycle," Xander muttered.

"Mom's flowers, Buffy," Dawn said softly.

There was nothing green left on Buffy's street. No grass, no shrubs, no flowers. The trees were skeletons. "If we're going to see how far this has spread, we're going to need the car. I'll get the keys," Buffy said. She trotted toward the house.

At the far end of the block Willow spotted a group of neighbors huddled together. "What do you think they're saying to one another?" she asked. "I mean, if you don't know about the Hellmouth, or demons, what do you think?"

"Insects, toxins, terrorism," Giles suggested. "The mind is adept at explaining the unexplainable."

"And I'm assuming we're all thinking Buffy's new best friend had something to do with this," Xander said. "I mean, new demon in town. Strange destruction of plant life. Doesn't sound like a coincidence to me." He pulled a leaf off the nearest tree and rolled it between his fingers. It crumbled into a fine brown dust.

Just a minute ago it was smooth, and green, and juicy with life, Willow thought.

"That's something of a leap," Giles replied. "But, of course, it's one of the possibilities."

"What do you think, Buff?" Xander called as she returned from the house. "Do you think Mr. His-eyes-were-so-blue did this?"

"Well, he did tell me it was going to be a beautiful day until 3:04 and it's now—" She checked her watch.

"Three-oh-seven, so with going into the house for keys and—"

"He told you he was going to turn the world brown at 3:04?" Willow asked as they climbed into the car.

"No, he just said . . ." Buffy seemed to realize everyone was staring at her. "Guess I forgot to mention that part. Anyway, I'm thinking Michael's been having himself some fun."

"One demon did all this? By himself?" Dawn asked. "But why?"

Buffy shrugged. "Maybe he hates plants."

"Why doesn't he just move out to the desert?" Xander asked, climbing into the backseat of Buffy's car. Willow got in from the other side so that Xander wouldn't have to be squished in the middle between her and Dawn. When Giles was around, it was just assumed that he got the front seat.

Willow stared through the window as they drove through town. You didn't really realize how much growing green stuff there was around, until it was gone.

Buffy made a sharp right into a tiny parking lot. "I think we need an even bigger picture. Come on."

They all piled out of the car behind her. Willow glanced up at the neon sign over the door: Bubba's Beer Barn. "Um, Buff?" she said. "A sports bar? Really?"

"I don't think this is the time for more drinking," Giles protested. "And there's Dawn. She won't be allowed in a bar."

"I don't think anyone's going to be checking IDs today," Buffy said.

And nobody did. All the clean-cut, gigantic college guys were gathered around the bar's big-screen TV. It was tuned to CNN—an unusual choice for a sports bar, Willow noted, but no one was complaining. The bar was silent, everyone listening intently to the grim-faced reporter standing in the Amazon. At least that's where she claimed to be; you couldn't tell by looking at the scene behind her. It was as barren as a desert.

The scrolling line of text below the reporter gave info about tornados in Egypt, ball lightning in England, and sandstorms in Canada.

One demon did all this, Willow thought, echoing Dawn. It would definitely take strong magick to fight him. She hoped she had it inside her, untainted.

"Seen enough?" Buffy asked Giles.

He nodded, and they made their way back through the growing crowd and out onto the sidewalk.

"Giles, how long do you think it will take before the destruction of all the plant life affects the oxygen supply?" Willow asked.

"The ozone layer should give us time for regrowth," he answered, seeming startled by the question.

"But what if it . . . Michael . . . never lets anything grow again?" Dawn asked, her eyes huge with worry.

"Not gonna happen," Xander answered. "You think Buffy can't handle that pretty boy with one hand tied behind her back?"

"I think we need to consider the possibility that he has comrades," Giles said.

Willow felt something wet on her cheek. *This is no time for crying,* she told herself sternly. Then she realized it wasn't a tear. It was a snowflake. A soft, wet, lacy snowflake.

It was snowing, in southern California, and summer was barely over. The pretty boy had struck again.

"I think we should get some food," Willow suggested as Buffy led the way down the grocery-store aisle. They were all decked out in mismatched winter ski clothes from Buffy's closet, and they'd decided to do an emergency blizzard-food run. Well, everyone except Giles, who'd remained at home to research deforestation.

Buffy stared pointedly into their shopping cart. "We've got seven boxes of hot cocoa mix, because everyone loves hot cocoa when it snows, or at least people on TV do. We've got sugar cookies, 'cause snow feels like Christmas, at least on TV. Xander's getting the Smacks. We've got chocolate and graham crackers, so we can make s'mores, and don't worry, I'm not going to forget the marshmallows." Even though they were all worried about the state of the world's environment, it was hard to be all doom and gloom during a snowstorm, especially if you'd only seen snow once before in your life, like Buffy. She just couldn't help feeling a certain amount of cheer in the face of danger.

"I meant *food* food. You know, nutritious stuff, in case we're snowed in for days and days. More like that woman." Willow pointed to a panic-stricken lady who had a cart filled with what looked like the entire canned food aisle.

Buffy wrinkled her nose. "Canned food gives me hives. Besides, as soon as the snow's gone we're going to dig ourselves out and beat this thing." Cheer wasn't even a good way to describe how she felt, Buffy decided. She felt confident, filled with strength . . . almost happy.

Willow grinned back at her. "Yeah!" she said. "Besides, we'll have marshmallows."

"Exactly," Buffy replied with a giggle. "Big ones for the s'mores and minis for the cocoa. They're at the end of this aisle, right next to Michael."

Michael. Buffy almost started to do the blinking thing again. There was something about that guy. . . . He was almost too perfect to be real. But he was real, and he was here, and he was smiling at her.

She started toward him, although she didn't remember giving her feet the order to move. "Michael. Hi."

"Hey, Buffy," he said. "I'm eating a Devil Dog. Have you ever had one?"

"Uh. Yeah." *Now what do I say?* she thought, smiling up at him.

"Good, huh?" Michael took another bite of the Devil Dog.

"Yeah. Good," Buffy managed to repeat. How was it possible that one guy could be so beautiful? And smart. She knew that they were having a really high-quality conversation here.

"Have a taste." He held the Devil Dog up to her lips and she automatically took a bite. It was like her senses had been turned up to eleven. *Wow. Chocolate. Cream filling. Fluorescent grocery store lights. Michael's eyes. The world is a beautiful, beautiful place.*

"Well, I have to go," Michael said. "See you."

"See you," Buffy managed to repeat.

Michael made every part of her, including her brain, turn to goo. Sweet, warm, happy goo. And that was bad. It was debil—what was the word? Bad. Very, very bad. Made Buffy bad Slayer. She giggled again.

Willow, Dawn, and Xander rushed up as soon as Michael turned the corner.

"If you get me that, I'll forget all about Mr. Happy," Dawn breathed. "*He'll* be my Mr. Happy."

"Is that him? Michael?" Willow asked, staring at the place where Michael once stood.

"He seems like a good guy," Xander said. "A really good guy."

"Yeah," Buffy repeated.

"Yeah," said Willow.

Buffy sighed, drawing in a breath of fetid air. She coughed. Something smelled. Glancing down, she realized she was standing in a puddle of unrecognizable pink stickiness. Someone must have spilled juice here or something.

She looked back up, blinking against the bright light. The fluorescent glow suddenly felt a little too harsh and ugly. In fact, there were lots of ugly things around. And lots of reasons to be worried. And no reason at all to be standing around eating Devil Dogs.

"Yeah," she said again. "He seems like a good guy—for someone who murders plants!"

She took off after Michael. He had turned right at the end of the aisle, but when she got there, he was gone. A quick scan of the checkout area showed her long lines of frightened people, but no Michael. He had vanished. Slowly she returned to her friends. They looked as if they'd just woken from a nice dream to find themselves mired in a not-so-nice reality.

"You guys, that was the demon," Buffy said. "Why didn't you haul me away from him?"

"Hey," Xander said defensively. "I'm not the one who was eating out of—"

Buffy pointed her finger in Xander's face. "Don't you say it," she ordered him.

"I guess his thrall thingy works on all of us," Willow said. "I was just too happy to want to attack him. I didn't even remember he was a demon."

"Me neither," Dawn put in. "I was just hoping he'd talk to me."

"Right," Xander said. "Me too."

"So he makes everyone feel entranced," Willow said. "Finding an antidote to that has to be first on our list of things to do."

"You got that right." Buffy grabbed a bag of spongy marshmallows. "I hate being an emotion puppet. I see him—I'm happy. But I don't even know him. It just happens." Frustrated, she gave the bag of marshmallows a twist. They felt way too soft—not spongy, but squishy. Almost wet. Buffy glanced at the bag with a frown.

"You look like you're gonna hurl," Dawn told Buffy.

Slowly Buffy held up the plastic bag. White maggots wriggled between the white marshmallows, turning the marshmallows into a slimy, moving bag of goo. She dropped the bag and kicked it across the linoleum floor.

Someone in the next aisle gave an ear-splitting shriek.

"Dawn, put the ice cream down," Willow ordered.

Buffy followed Willow's gaze. The pints of ice cream Dawn held cradled against her chest were writhing. Dawn let out a yelp and flung them away from herself. The top fell off the chocolate chocolate chip, and there were as many maggots inside as chips.

From all over the store came the sounds of people screaming and merchandise being thrown to the ground. Buffy couldn't take her eyes from the wriggling bag of marshmallows.

"I'd like to say something clever," Xander said, "but let's just run!"

"Yikes!" Willow cried as a wave made up of melted snow lifted her off her feet. She would have gone down if she, Xander, Buffy, and Dawn weren't linking arms, forming a wall against the water rushing down the street as they headed home.

"How hot do you think it must be, to have melted all that snow so fast?" Dawn asked. "I mean, it must've been eight feet high when we left the grocery store."

"Hot enough to have given you an insta-sunburn," Buffy told her. "It's giving me ouchies just looking at you."

Dawn seemed to have been cured of her pissy-itis,

Willow observed. The world turning weird would usually do that for you, strip off the unimportant stuff. And now Willow didn't need her prickles to tell her there was weirdness brewing in Sunnydale. Everybody knew it. The question that was pounding through her with every beat of her heart was how soon it would be until she had to use her magicks to fight it. And what would happen when she did?

"Get ready to turn, troops," Xander called out. "Buffy's driveway approacheth."

Willow fought against the knee-high water until she was facing Buffy's house. The front door swung open as they struggled toward it. Giles stood waiting for them, his arms loaded down with towels. Watchers were kind of like the Boy Scouts with that always-be-prepared thing.

"What did you find out?" Buffy asked when they reached him. "I want to stop being happy! Today!"

"I haven't been able to find out much as yet, I'm afraid," Giles admitted.

"Oooh, I'll help," Willow cried, doing everything but raising her hand and begging "pick me, pick me, pick me." Research she could handle, and she was good at it. And it was useful.

And it's safe, she added to herself. *Be honest. That's the big attraction. It's safe.*

"Excellent, Willow, thank you," Giles answered.

Willow rushed upstairs, got into some dry clothes, and then sat down in one of her favorite places in the world—in front of a computer keyboard. Buffy,

Xander, and Giles were confabbing on the sofa. *Okay,* she thought, ignoring them for now. *I want a way to neutralize the thrall of a demon who—*

The front door opened with a bang, jerking Willow away from her thoughts. Anya strode inside, wearing a handkerchief top, a short skirt, and a lot of sweat. Willow shot a look at Xander to see how he was reacting to the woman he had left at the altar looking so hot—in both senses of the word.

Anya turned toward Giles. "Welcome back," she snapped. "What the hell is going on around here? First it was hail, then it was gorgeous, then snowy, now Sahara but with the wet."

"Thanks for the recap," Xander muttered.

"It's very bad for the skin," Anya continued. "Do you have anything to eat around here? I'm starving."

"You can look," Buffy answered. "Maybe the food here is okay."

Anya headed for the kitchen. Xander hesitated, then followed. *Poor Xander,* Willow thought. *There's really no way he can make it up to Anya.*

"What did you mean about the food?" Giles asked.

"Big bad at the grocery store," Buffy explained. "Maggots everywhere. All the food was squishy."

"Well, here in the fridge of Chez Buffy we've got a choice of maggots or maggots," Xander called from the kitchen.

"Let's check the cupboards," Dawn suggested as she trotted down the stairs in shorts and a pink T-shirt. She disappeared into the kitchen.

"You have all this, Willow? Odd weather phenomena? Maggot infestation? Destruction of vegetation?" Giles asked.

"Yes, yes, and yes," Willow answered, biting her tongue so she wouldn't add a "duh." She'd been there, remember? But she knew Giles was just thinking out loud, trying to see some connection.

"Our demon's an eclectic fellow," Giles muttered. "Likes variety in his mayhem."

"What demon?" Anya called from the kitchen.

"Blond, blue eyes, beautiful, makes you feel all warm and cozy," Buffy answered, as Anya appeared in the living room.

"And, oh yeah, is attempting to destroy our supplies of oxygen and food," Xander added from the kitchen. "I'm not sure his affect on Buffy has completely worn off."

"Well, I've had a double exposure," Buffy protested. "The rest of you only saw him once."

Willow kept working the computer. She was good at this. Please couldn't she just sit here all day and solve the badness from right here?

"Does any of this sound familiar to you, Anya?" Giles asked. "He may be working alone or as part of a team. There have been global consequences."

Anya shrugged. "Vengeance demons don't tend to hang out with the ones that make you feel warm and cozy," she said.

"So you don't know Michael," Dawn called from the other room. Willow had a feeling Dawn had just wanted an excuse to say his name. Even now, she herself felt a little tingly when she remembered what Michael looked like. It hadn't been any kind of sexual feeling that she'd experienced standing in the grocery store with him. It had just been . . . happiness.

"Well, we've got to neutralize his thrall," Giles said. "It's imperative that we find a way for Buffy to get close to this demon without getting—"

"I have a basic anti-guy charm," Anya interrupted. "It stops anything male from putting anything over on anything female." She tossed a silver chain with an onyx ball over to Buffy. "I want that back," she said before she headed back into the kitchen.

Willow shot a doubtful look at Giles. He shrugged. "The creature *is* male."

Buffy put on the necklace. "And I'm female. It might work. I guess I might as well start with a basic patrol. Michael seems good at finding me wherever I am."

"You want backup?" Xander asked, coming back into the living room.

"Nah, only one necklace," Buffy told him. "And it's not like you didn't feel anything when you were around the blondie. Didn't you say he was a '*really good guy*'?"

A flush rose up Xander's neck and he disappeared back into the kitchen.

As Buffy left the house Willow wanted to call out a warning to be careful. But it seemed redundant when you were demon hunting.

There was a clatter from the kitchen. "Maggots," Anya spat out.

"The canned stuff isn't any good either," Dawn called. "And . . . oh, gross." She rushed into the living room. "I'm not hungry anymore."

"Okay, I have a demon whose breath causes maggot infestations. The maggots eat everything that's dead first, then move on to the living," Willow announced. "But a cross-ref with uncharacteristic weather patterns and plant killing turns up nothing," she added quickly. "So, not our guy."

"I'm disappointed," Xander admitted, returning to the room. "I kind of like fighting the small, soft, and brainless."

"These maggots could be controlled by the demon to work as a unit," Willow explained. "And they could each eat a thousand times their weight per—"

"But that demon's not our guy," Xander interrupted, beginning to itch his back with both hands.

"No," she assured him. "I also found an ancient curse that involves an escalating weather pattern where it gets hotter and hotter until the sun explodes, basically, you know—"

"Destroying the earth," Giles finished for her.

Willow nodded. "But no food ickiness in that one, so—"

"Twinkies!" Anya cried gleefully. "Oh, Twinkies!" She danced into the living room clutching a box of Twinkies to her chest. She ripped the cellophane off one of the pastries and stuffed half of it in her mouth.

"Ew! Oh, ew, ew!" Dawn exclaimed. She buried her head in her hands.

"We may all have to consider this course of action

at some point," Giles commented, his eyes locked on the small white thing at the corner of Anya's mouth. "Insects are an excellent source of protein."

Anya noticed the direction of his gaze. "Cream filling. Duh." She licked the dab of filling away. "I found a maggot-free food! Twinkies!"

"Everyone always said roaches could survive the end of the world. And now we know what they'll be living on. Twinkies," Xander observed. "Well, actually, the vast array of tasty chemical preservatives that are Twinkies."

Willow added the info about Twinkies to her search. *Give me something,* she silently prayed. *Something that doesn't involve using magick.*

If she had to use her powers . . . Her stomach gave a lurch. She looked over at Giles, knowing just seeing his face would bring her comfort.

But she saw him sprawled on the sofa—dead.

Anya on the floor—dead.

Xander. Oh, god. A piece of meat. Veins and flesh, just like Warren without his skin. No Xander left.

Dawnie, little Dawnie. Willow couldn't even look.

It's your fear. You're seeing your fear, she told herself, forcing her eyes back to her computer screen. But she couldn't escape the truth. She had a very good reason to be afraid.

CHAPTER FOUR

Buffy headed to the side entrance of the cemetery, the entrance closest to the creek that ran through it. She could hear the rushing water from half a block away. All that melted snow and hail had found a good home, she thought.

The gate on this side of the cemetery was always locked, so Buffy scaled it. She prowled through the tombstones, fingering Anya's necklace. She'd find Michael soon, she knew it. There was some kind of connection between them, and this time she'd use that to her advantage. Buffy reached the body of water that was once the creek, wider than usual by at least twenty feet. And across the rushing white water, almost as if he had known she was coming, stood Michael.

"Buffy, hi!" he shouted over the creek.

Buffy's heart began to beat faster, and it felt as if she'd gotten an injection of sweet, warm honey. Michael. It was Michael. Her hand went to Anya's necklace, and she was vaguely aware that it was supposed to be doing something.

Michael was watching her with a slightly confused smile.

Buffy's weapons bag began to slide off her shoulder, forgotten. Her skin tingled with life, and happiness shot through her. Michael's eyes met hers, and she let herself sink into the impossible blueness of them. So blue she could see the color even this far away. Then something inside her snapped, like a bone breaking. The happiness was gone, replaced by stark reality. "Thanks, Anya," she whispered.

Michael held a large clay bowl shaped somewhat like a conch shell out over the rushing water.

A bolt of white-hot fury rushed through Buffy's body. No more cozy, buttery, bubble bath feeling for her. This demon had done enough. It was time to kill him.

"Bridge. A bridge would be nice right now," she said, scanning the banks of the creek. It was far too wide to jump and moving far too quickly to swim across. But it wasn't absolutely necessary to get all up close and personal to fight. She emptied her leather bag on the muddy ground in front of her. "Projectile. Something that projects," she murmured as she studied her choices.

Her eyes lit on a crossbow. Perfect. She snatched it

up and loaded a nice, heavy iron arrow. Then she took aim at Michael's heart. The heart was a good target for any creature. And somehow she couldn't make herself take aim at that beautiful face.

Buffy pulled the trigger. The bow recoiled into her shoulder with a satisfying thud. The arrow shot across the river, flying toward Michael with perfect aim.

Then it stopped. It stopped inches away from him, quivering in the empty air. Michael didn't react at all.

Fine. I'm just getting started, Buffy thought. She'd brought along everything she could carry, including a miniature catapult. She grabbed the closest weapon—a mace. Well, technically it was called a spiked flail, as Giles was always telling her. But as long as it killed things, she didn't care what its name was. She gripped the wooden handle hard and swung it over her head, the chain whipping in a vicious circle. When the spiked metal ball at the end of the chain had reached its greatest momentum, Buffy let the handle go. The ball whined as it sped through the air toward Michael. *This one's going to do it,* Buffy had time to think—before the flail took its place in the air next to the arrow.

Without allowing herself to break her rhythm, Buffy caught up her long-handled spear, reared back, and flung it with all her might. Then she spun three ninja throwing stars across the river one after the other, *zing, zing, zing.*

This time Michael looked up and gave her a little wave. He didn't seem bothered by the growing wall of artillery hanging in the air in front of him, not even when Buffy added five stakes, a butcher knife, a battle ax, and a katana sword.

Okay, let's see what else we can play with, Buffy thought. She looked down at the ground and realized she had nothing left. Not that it mattered, because with a couple of thunks and a clatter, all her weapons fell to the ground at Michael's feet. He didn't touch them.

Buffy bent her knees slightly, getting into attack position. Her eyes scanned Michael's body as she tried to get some sense of what his next move was going to be. *Does he have the ability to leap over the river? Does he—*

Michael snapped the large clay bowl in two, and the low, mournful sound of a whale's cry filled the air. Buffy jumped back, startled. He dropped both halves of the bowl into the river, and then he turned and walked away. *That was anticlimactic,* she thought.

Buffy stomped up to the edge of the river. "Hey!" she yelled, planting her hands on her hips. "You can't just . . . throw things in the water and walk away! Get back here and fight me like a—"

The churning of the water grew more frantic, and the white foam turned to green as a gigantic head rose up inches away from Buffy's face. Huge razor-sharp fangs filled her entire field of vision.

". . . sea monster," she finished weakly, as she thought longingly of her whole stash of weapons lying on the opposite shore.

The sea monster reared higher, its dragon head poised over Buffy. It opened its jaws, and she could smell its breath, like sushi that had been left out of the fridge for a couple of days.

Buffy backed up a few steps. The monster kept its eyes on her, swaying back and forth on its thick column of a body, like a cobra preparing to strike. She took another step back and felt the solid granite of a tombstone against her calf. *Found me a weapon,* she thought. In one fast motion she spun around, already crouching, and wrenched the gravestone out of the earth.

"Okay, look at me, all pink and tasty," Buffy crooned to the monster. "You know you want it." The creature's massive pupils narrowed, and a thick strand of saliva dripped from its jaws. It began to sway a little more quickly.

Buffy forced herself to stand still. She couldn't throw the tombstone at that disgusting head; it wouldn't do enough damage. She needed the head to come to her. "Come on, just a little closer," she coaxed.

The head whipped down. Buffy leapt out of its path and swung the tombstone into the side of the sea monster's face with all her might. A brown, viscous liquid squirted out, spraying her cheek, and the monster let out a hiss. Buffy didn't give the monster a chance to retaliate. She slammed the tombstone into it again, aiming for the spot that was already injured. The monster gave another hiss of pain. Pain and anger. Buffy realized it wasn't even close to death.

It began to rear up. She couldn't let it get its huge mouth over her. As the sea monster rose on its snake-like body, Buffy leapt onto its humongous head. It roared out in protest, and Buffy's mouth, nose, and lungs were filled with the rotten stink of its breath.

While the creature's mouth was open, Buffy slid forward as far as she could, and then she held on with her knees and used both hands to bring the tombstone down onto the sea monster's closest fang. It took three swings, but then Buffy had a new weapon: the freshly extracted fang, sharp and lethal as any sword she'd used.

The sea monster shook its head viciously, trying to hurl Buffy to the ground where it could reach her. "I'm sorry," Buffy said. "I should have given you painkillers before I pulled the tooth. I think this will help."

She raised the tooth over her head and plunged it into the monster's brain. The creature screamed. Buffy hung on tight as its entire body flailed and bucked, then went still.

Buffy turned and saw that the dead sea monster reached from one side of the river to the other. "Cool," she said. "Got myself a bridge." After quickly retrieving her bag of weapons, she trotted over the creature's slimy back. Maybe Michael could stop a weapon in midair, but could he stop a fist? She was aching to find out. She strode through the graveyard, her feet making a sucking sound with every step in the muddy ground. She hated that sound: *suck, suck, suck.*

Buffy froze, listening. Yeah, there it was. A suck that hadn't come from one of her feet. Someone was behind her. She pulled a stake out of the waistband of her jeans.

She turned fast, knees bent, and saw a woman coming toward her. Undead, definitely. Pieces of rotting cloth were sliding off her skin, and pieces of rotting skin were sliding off her bones. Buffy could see every detail, every ragged vein and deteriorating muscle, because the woman's entire body was glowing with a soft, lightning-bug phosphorescence.

"Pretty," Buffy murmured. Then she wrinkled her nose. She couldn't believe the word "pretty" had come out of her mouth. Yeah, she'd seen uglier things than the woman's decaying body—much, much uglier things. But even compared to them, "pretty" was not the word she'd use to describe the zombie. But that glowiness . . .

Buffy realized she'd let the zombie walk right by her. "We have plenty of electric lights, thank you very much," Buffy said as she chased after the zombie, raised her stake, and brought it down into the woman's flesh, right between two of the ties holding the back of her funeral dress together.

The zombie kept walking without hesitation, her high-heeled pumps slurping in the mud, the stake embedded in her body. "All righty, then. You want to go the full ten rounds," Buffy muttered.

"Watch yourself," a voice called out.

"Thanks for the assist," Buffy answered, recognizing the voice, recognizing it in her flesh and bones. Would it always be that way now?

"You can't kill them. I already bloody tried," Spike said from behind her. "Anyway, far as I can tell, the ones that glow are harmless dimwits."

Buffy stared after the zombie woman. She realized the zombie was heading toward a ring of soft light in the distance. "How many of them are there?" She sprang forward without waiting for an answer.

Spike grabbed her by the elbow, and her skin remembered being touched by him in exactly that place. This had to stop. She didn't want him. She didn't want to remember wanting him.

"Did you not hear me tell you to watch yourself?" Spike asked. "There are open graves from here to jack all."

Buffy shook off his hand, then scanned the muddy ground. He was right. Grave after grave had been left a gaping hole.

"I was just taking a look at the old digs," Spike told her. "One minute I'm down in the crypt, minding my own business. The next minute the earth opens up, the top of the crypt rips off, and I'm sucked right out! Like a bloody sardine being slurped out of a tin."

"Weird," Buffy commented. "Did you see anything useful?" She stepped up to the edge of the closest grave and peered down at it. The coffin inside had been shattered into pieces of wood the size of matches.

"Just the walking glowsticks," Spike answered. "And the ones like him." He jerked his chin toward a man crouched behind the tombstone at the end of the row. The man was in the same basic condition as the woman, maybe underground a year or so longer, Buffy decided. But no glow.

"Now, he wants killin' if you ask me. Seems to be your basic zombie. Useless. Lurches about feeding on people's brains. Doesn't really talk, forget about playing a hand of poker," Spike commented.

He ran his fingers through his white-blond hair. "I would say that we should be rounding up the brain-eaters first, but I don't like that over there." He nodded at the circle of light. "Looks like someone's getting the glowies together. They aren't smart enough to do it on their own. I don't like the idea of them getting organized."

"Yeah, I wouldn't want them starting a bake sale or anything," Buffy said as she carefully made her way between two of the open graves, heading toward the light. "The PTA would be all over my butt."

She heard Spike start after her. "I don't need a chaperone," she called without turning.

"This is extreme magick, Slayer," he answered, and kept on coming. "Raising the dead and all. Not to mention the plants dying off, and the weather disturbance."

"It's just another demon with a sick sense of what's fun, Spike," Buffy told him.

She kept her eyes on the ground, making sure to plant her feet on solid mud with each step. Mud, mud, mud, foot. Her eyes rested on a man's foot wearing a lace-up shoe, except the laces had been mostly eaten by something. The foot wasn't glowing. Buffy's eyes traveled up the leg attached to the foot. No glow. This was a brain-eater.

I hate fighting in the mud, Buffy thought. *No traction.* She leapt into the air and kicked out with one high-heeled boot.

"Nice," Spike commented when her heel connected with what was left of the zombie's nose. The zombie went down and Spike shoved it into the nearest grave. "Stay!" he ordered it.

The group of human glowsticks was closer now, and Buffy was able to pick up her pace because their light made it easier to run the graveyard maze. She paused when she realized that the glowing zombies were gathered around a dark figure. It raised its arms, and a sucking sound broke the silence. Buffy's ears popped, like they did on a plane making a descent.

A spray of dirt and dead grass arched over the heads of the zombies—dirt, dead grass, and slivers of metal. The zombies' soft golden glow reflected off the silver, and for a moment it looked like a metallic star shower.

"Looks like it was an Emperor's Slumber," Spike commented. "The cash blokes pay for boxes to get themselves buried in . . ."

Buffy nodded. The pieces of metal were from a very high-end Emperor-brand coffin. A coffin that had just shattered like brittle glass.

The glowies moved over to the next grave, still covered with dirt and dead grass, while a young man—not much decay, no glow—clawed his way out of the newly opened grave. He rubbed away the glue holding his eyelids shut and stared around, looking confused, terrified, and betrayed.

Project much? Buffy asked herself.

Spike put his hand on her shoulder, as if he knew what she was thinking. As if he knew she was reliving that moment, clawing out of her own grave. Going from unexplainable beauty and peace to . . . no one there to explain.

"That one guy who's doing the sucking? I've got to see this . . . sucker," Buffy announced, although she had a very strong suspicion of who it was. She strode forward to get away from Spike's touch, to get away from her memories of death. She pushed her way through the group of glowies. Their flesh was cool, no heat in the light coming off it.

Spike followed at her heels. But as they got closer to the dark figure, he began to whimper.

"What's with you?" Buffy asked, glancing at him. Spike's gaze was locked on something over her shoulder. Correction: some*one*. He stared at the being in the center of the circle, eyes filled with fear.

"Spike?" Buffy said.

He screamed like a frightened animal, the sound sending Buffy's heart slamming into her throat. Before she could ask what he'd seen, Spike turned and ran. Buffy was shocked. When was the last time she'd seen Spike run from a fight? Buffy ignored the question and fought her way into the center of the circle.

"Hey, Buffy," Michael said, his hands raised over the next grave. He smiled at her.

She smiled back. "Hey, way-too-pretty-boy-whose-hobby-is-making-zombies." *This is going to feel so good,* she thought. Buffy launched a roundhouse kick, aiming at Michael's ribs.

The sensation was completely unexpected. It was like hitting the punching bag she used in practice— muffled, muted. Michael's turtleneck was tight. And so was his body. But what she felt was not body-to-body impact.

Buffy didn't take the time to think about it. She spun around and followed up with a punch to the jaw. There was no crack of bone connecting to bone, just that feeling of her fist hitting a practice bag.

She swung with her other fist, this time keeping her eyes locked on her hand. She didn't even touch him. He hadn't even bothered to flinch. Something stopped her fist before it made contact. An invisible something, like a soft wall around Michael.

Just because it's invisible doesn't mean I can't smash through it, Buffy thought, and she went at it with every move she'd ever learned. She used fists, knees, elbows, fingernails. She tried to leap over it. She tried to slither under it on her belly.

Scraped, bruised, and breathless, she hurled herself at the barrier with a full-body slam. The impact threw her back on the ground.

Michael stared down at her, the glowies watching impassively. His brow furrowed over his light blue eyes. "What are you doing, Buffy?" he asked, his melting voice all concern and compassion. "Don't you know you can't fight me?"

CHAPTER FIVE

"**G**iles, what the hell is going on?" Buffy demanded as she burst into the living room. "You never told me there's something I can't fight."

Giles, Dawn, Xander, and Willow looked up from their research session. With a glance Giles took in all the new cuts and bruises on his Slayer. He should be used to it, but it always pained him. "Well, Buffy—," he began.

Of course she interrupted him. "No, you don't understand. I couldn't even touch him! He had a force field thingy."

"Yes, but what—," Giles asked, struggling to get the essential information.

"I mean, Anya's charm worked. I wasn't under his

spell. I wanted to kill him, Giles. And I couldn't."

"Well, that's—"

"Giles, stop arguing with me," Buffy said, cutting him off. He'd never been able to break her of her interruption habit. "This demon is sucking people out of graves. And making them glow. And did I mention he has a force field thingy? What are we—"

"Buff, it might be helpful if you left a little space in between your rants for Giles to insert an answer," Xander cut in.

Giles gave him a thankful smile. "Well, I appreciate the suggestion, but I'm afraid in this case I don't have an immediate course of action planned. Buffy, could you describe the force field?"

"I punched, kicked, did everything you trained me to do, and I never connected. Not once," Buffy answered.

"I'm more worried about the glowing dead people. Sounds like zombies. Is he raising an army, do you think?" Xander jumped in.

Buffy turned to him. "There *were* a whole bunch of them gathered around Michael. Like they were worshipping him or something. Maybe he's planning to use them for . . . whatever he's going to do next."

Giles opened his mouth to speak.

"Oh! And he called up a sea monster. But I killed it," Buffy added in a rush.

Giles waited for a moment. Was she finished? Buffy raised her eyebrows impatiently. Ah. She was finished.

"So you are able to fight his minions," Giles said.

All eyes in the room were on him. He knew that when he wasn't here they managed on their own. But when he was back, they reverted to their old roles, himself included, and he had to admit a part of him enjoyed it. "I think that since for the moment we haven't discovered how to attack Michael himself, we should concentrate on these zombies. How many were there?"

"Hundreds!" Buffy answered. "Almost all the graves in that cemetery are empty. It happened all of a sudden, while Michael and I were fighting."

"Oh, Buffy, no!" Dawn exclaimed.

"Could you fight them?" Xander asked.

"Some of them," Buffy replied. "But there was this one that I tried to kill . . ." She frowned at a spot of gray-green foam on the sleeve of her jacket. "She barely even noticed me."

"How'd you do it?" Xander pressed.

"Stake in the back."

"Okay, that's the problem. With zommers, you have to go for the head. You don't have to chop it off, but you've got to destroy the frontal lobe—you didn't stake the frontal lobe, did you?"

Giles and the others stared at him. "Um, no," Buffy admitted.

"See, that would have worked," Xander continued. "That, or a baseball bat, nail gun, anything. Burning also works. The literature isn't definitive on whether they can swim."

Willow looked up from the computer and cracked

her knuckles. "By literature, I'm sure you all know he means comic books."

"And movies," Xander added.

"Well, I did kill one by kicking in his nose," Buffy said. "Some of the zombies glow, and I couldn't kill them. The ones that don't glow? Back to dead."

Giles shot Willow a look. "I'll switch over to zombie research," she said. He nodded.

The front door opened and Anya staggered through, loaded down with more boxes of Twinkies than he'd imagined one small woman, er, vengeance demon, could carry. "Some help would be nice," she said, her voice muffled by the boxes, which were stacked so high they blocked her mouth.

Xander was instantly on his feet, Dawn only a second behind him. Giles suspected they had slightly different motives.

"What's going on?" Anya demanded as soon as the Twinkies were safe. "There are dead people wandering all over the place. And demons everywhere you turn."

"Demons?" Buffy asked.

"Yeah, they're all leaving town," Anya answered. "Always a bad sign."

"I think I should talk to some of them. Could be there's some gossip out there about Michael," Buffy said. She was clearly eager to take action of any kind. Giles knew how much Buffy hated being idle when there was danger at hand.

"Go," he told her. Buffy was out the door a moment later.

"Peel me one of those," Anya ordered Xander, jerking her head toward the closest box of Twinkies.

"Hey, I'm not your houseboy anymore," he protested weakly.

"I foraged, you peel," she insisted. He ripped open a box, and stripped the cellophane off one of the cakes and handed it to her.

"You want one, Giles?" Xander asked.

"I'm certain I will never be that hungry," Giles answered. "Now, why don't you—"

The door opened with a bang. Spike rushed in and planted himself directly in front of Giles. "What the bloody hell is going on? You never told me there was a demon I couldn't fight."

Even vampires older than I am expect me to play nursemaid, Giles thought. "Well, Spike—," he began.

"You don't understand," Spike interrupted, proving many years of life experience did not guarantee good manners. "I couldn't even touch this thing. He had this, this—"

"Force field thingy?" Xander volunteered, mouth full of Twinkie.

"Yes! Exactly!" Spike burst out.

"We know—," Giles said.

"Stop arguing with me. This thing was sucking people out of the ground. And making them glow."

"Shut up, Spike!" Dawn snapped. "Let Giles talk."

"Thank you," Giles answered, then wondered if he should have praised her rudeness. But he shouldn't be expected to teach everyone everything. "Now, Spike, what can you tell us about this demon?"

"He was the most hideous thing I've ever seen," Spike replied.

"That can't have been Michael," Willow commented, her fingers still flying over the keyboard. "He's gorgeous."

"Well, I don't know the creature's name, but I know he was hideous," Spike replied. "Ask Buffy. I was with her when we saw him."

Giles sighed. Buffy had told him about Spike's odd behavior ever since he had gotten his soul back. Apparently the vampire had gone somewhat mad. He was at best an unreliable witness.

"What about the zombies?" Giles asked. "Anything you can tell us about them?"

"Giles, I think you should have a look at this." Willow turned the laptop toward him and clicked a button, and a somewhat jerky newscast began to play. Quarantines were in place in Peru, Africa, and Mexico to contain an as-yet-unidentified disease. Giles felt the muscles in his throat convulse when he heard the symptoms: flesh rotting, problems with motor skills, and psychological disorders. Clearly what people saw as disease was actually zombie outbreaks.

"I'm thinking this might be a little too big for the Scoobies to handle with baseball bats and nail guns," Xander said.

Giles shot a look a Willow.

"So I'm back to researching the force field thingy," she said.

He nodded confirmation. It was a pleasure to work with her, they so rarely needed words.

"I'll gather up some hammers and bats and high-heeled shoes," Xander announced. "Just in case a few of the zoms try to storm our headquarters."

Buffy stepped into the diner. It was empty except for Michael. In fact, most places were empty now. People were either hiding at home or they'd simply left town, although judging from the newscast Willow had shown her when she got home, leaving town wasn't going to help. The whole world was falling apart.

Michael sat in a booth by the window, holding a mug of what looked like hot cocoa. Outside a cluster of the glowing zombies stood staring in at him. Buffy smoothed down her flowered shirt, making sure her stake was tucked securely into the waistband of her black pants, and pasted a smile on her face.

The gang had found a way for her to break down Michael's force field. At least, they thought they had. It involved staying very calm and focused for the next few minutes. Not her strong point as the Slayer, but with Anya's necklace Buffy was sure she could pull it off. She and Giles had practiced the meditation of the ancient Indonesian warriors for more than three hours until she knew that she had almost peaked. Now, here in the diner with Michael, she would be at her best. She had to be. She had only one chance, this one time when he wasn't expecting her attack.

"He likes you," Willow had said as Buffy was getting ready to go. "He walked you home. With umbrella. And he fed you chocolate. It'll be like taking candy from a baby." Anya had made her change into a push-up bra before she left, even though Buffy had never gotten the feeling that Michael liked her *that* way.

Spike had glared at her, disapproval coming off him like a bad smell. And Dawn had given Buffy an extra-hard hug. Now here she was.

Buffy walked over and slid into the booth seat across from him. "If you didn't want to be found, you should have ditched your fans. They're lighting up the whole street with that glow." *I probably could have started things out a little more nicely,* she thought. *But it would probably have seemed suspicious if I acted too nice. After all, I was throwing punches the last time I saw him.*

"I'm always happy to see you, Buffy."

Buffy gritted her teeth at his sweetness. It would help to have him a little off balance before she started. "Well, before you get too friendly, first I should tell you that I killed your giant sea monkey," she announced.

"Why'd you do that?" Michael asked. He didn't sound mad or anything, just curious. He took a sip of his hot cocoa and smiled as if it was the best thing he'd ever tasted.

"Because its breath offended me," Buffy shot back. "Why'd you kill all the plants in sight? Green not your color? Why'd you start making zombies? Feeling lonely?"

"Would you like some hot cocoa?" Michael asked.

Buffy sighed. He wasn't easy to goad into any kind

of emotion. She glanced at the steaming cocoa in his mug. "No maggots?" she asked.

"No maggots," he promised. Buffy nodded, and Michael headed to the kitchen.

She pulled a deep breath and pretended she was back in the kitchen with Giles. "'First picture a flower with silver petals,'" she heard him say in her mind, and she had her flower back, the same one she'd called up when they practiced. A magnolia with large, strong petals, metallic silver instead of white.

Michael returned, slid his cute little butt back in the booth, and set a mug of hot cocoa with extra whipped cream—damn him—in front of Buffy. She didn't taste it. Instead, as she held the picture of her silver magnolia in her head, she tried to calculate where Michael's force field was. She tried to remember how far away her weapons had stopped in front of him, how close her fist had come to his face before it made that dull thud. *I figure it's about halfway across the table,* she thought.

"Don't you like whipped cream?" Michael asked. He flicked his finger in the whipped cream of Buffy's hot cocoa and licked it clean.

Okay, now make the flower spin, Buffy instructed herself. "I want you out of my town," she burst out, using her anger to hurl the metal flower around and around. "I want you gone, and I want you to take all your dead friends with you, and I want it to happen now. Because if you stay, I will find a way to destroy you." The flower in Buffy's mind spun faster and faster. The petals turned to blades sharp as razors. "I promise you that."

Go! Go! Go! With a mental scream Buffy let the razor flower fly toward Michael's force field. For a moment she saw it. She saw a ball of pulsing, shimmering gold surrounding Michael as her small, multi-bladed flower bounced off it, sparks flying. Then the gold ball and the flower disappeared.

"Won't you stop trying to fight me, Buffy?" Michael said, leaning across the table toward her. "It's impossible, don't you know that?" He reached out and touched the necklace Anya had loaned her, the one with the charm guaranteed to keep guys from playing girls. "This doesn't work on me either, by the way."

Buffy snorted. "Then why do I hate you so much right now?"

His smile dimmed a little. "I just saw you wearing it earlier and I realized what you were trying to do. So I turned it off. I would have done it before if I knew it bothered you. I never thought someone wouldn't enjoy feeling pleasure."

"You turned what off?" Buffy asked.

"I don't know what to call it. It is something I exude that people find joyful," Michael answered. "The charm doesn't affect me. But it made me realize that you—"

"That I prefer free will?" Buffy shot back.

"Yes. But others need my . . . comfort. During the end time, there's a great need for reassurance," Michael said, his blue eyes beaming sincerity.

"The end time?" Buffy repeated. *Okay, this sounds like a good track to follow. Might as well get some info while I'm here.* "What's that?"

"The end. The end of the world," Michael said simply.

Buffy's breath caught in her throat, but she forced herself to give the appearance of calm. So he wanted to end the world? She'd stopped other demons from doing that before. A strange sense of peace settled over her. Now she knew what she was facing. Now it was obvious what had to be done. "So, you're here to end the world?" she asked conversationally.

"It's my job," he answered.

"Your job," Buffy repeated. "And what exactly is your job? No, let's back it up a step. Who are you?"

"I'm Michael."

Buffy closed her eyes for a long moment, then opened them. "O-kay. Michael. I got that. And, Michael, *what* are you?" If she could find out what kind of demon he was, she and Giles and the Scoobies could figure out how to take him down.

"I'm an angel."

Anya didn't like dead people. They smelled funny. And she'd never met one who could carry on any sort of interesting conversation. Well, except vampires. They were technically dead people, but she tended to put them in a different category from the zombies and other assorted reanimated corpses.

These glowing zombies didn't smell as bad as zombies usually smelled, though. But she still didn't like them. For one thing, they were blocking her view of the diner, where Buffy had gone to talk to the demon.

No one had asked Anya to keep an eye on the Slayer. In fact, no one had asked her to do anything. Their big plan had involved all kinds of research—even Xander was involved in the zombie research. But no one had thought to ask Anya for help. Ever since she'd become a vengeance demon again, they acted as if she weren't part of their group. Sometimes it bothered her, and sometimes she liked it that way. But tonight she'd felt hurt when they excluded her. After all, she'd been trying to help ever since the new demon showed up. She'd gone Twinkie hunting, and she'd loaned Buffy her lying-man-repelling necklace. But no one had even noticed when she left.

So she'd followed Buffy into town. Maybe the Slayer would need backup. Anya pushed her way through another layer of glowing zombies. She knew she wouldn't be much help to Buffy. If she was being honest with herself, she'd admit that she'd mainly come here out of boredom. And if Buffy got into trouble, Anya could transport herself back to the others with a warning and look like a hero. It was a win-win situation.

"Move!" she growled in frustration. All these zombies were just staring at the diner. Something interesting must be going on inside. But they were too stupid to get out of her way. Anya dropped to her hands and knees and crawled forward. Was Buffy fighting with this Michael demon? Why were the zombies so interested?

Finally she saw the wall of the building through the glowing legs. Anya reached up and chopped one of the zombies behind the knee. It went down like a falling tree, and Anya stood up in its vacated spot.

She had a great view of the diner window. Buffy sat at a booth right inside with a blond-haired, blue-eyed monster. Icy fear gripped Anya so hard that she wasn't sure her lungs were actually working to bring air into her body. Buffy was just chatting with the hideous thing. The zombies were staring at it with big dumb smiles on their faces.

But it was horrible! Everything Anya had seen as a vengeance demon—bodies torn limb from limb, skulls crushed, eyes pecked out—paled in comparison with the hideousness of this demon. A small whimper escaped her lips. She'd never been so afraid in her thousand-plus years of life.

Get away from it! she told herself frantically. *Get out of here before it sees you!*

Anya was so terrified that she could barely remember how to use her powers. *Transport,* she thought. *Go back to where Xander is.* Trembling from head to foot, she transported herself.

"An angel," Buffy repeated.

Michael lowered his eyes to the table and gave a modest smile. "Archangel, actually."

Buffy massaged her temples. "An angel that creates zombies and sea monsters and turns plants to dust. Right," Buffy replied. But Michael's eyes, those light blue eyes . . . there wasn't any dishonesty in them.

You've seen demons with pretty faces before, she reminded herself.

But her heart believed Michael. Her mind couldn't stop it.

"I'm not doing these things because I want to. I must bring about the apocalypse," Michael clarified. "It's my duty. Just as Slayerhood has been your duty. We're on the same side, Buffy."

She forced herself to shake her head. "I save people. You're planning to destroy the world."

"We're both following the role we've been given by God," Michael told her, staring into her eyes.

"God. God? I don't . . . I don't really do the God thing," Buffy answered. She picked up the now-cool hot cocoa and took a long drink so she wouldn't have to look at him anymore.

"God, destiny, Buddha, fate, Mother Earth, higher power, Krishna, The Powers That Be, greater good, Grateful Dead, the Force . . ." Michael smiled. "It doesn't matter what people call it. Whatever made you the Slayer made me what I am and gave me the job I have to do."

"So you haven't had any face-to-face chats with God?" Buffy asked.

"No," he said. "I don't know who the decision-maker is any more than you do. I just know what my job is."

"And you're okay with that?" Buffy demanded. How could he be? How could this being that exuded peace and joy be okay with killing everything?

"Are you okay with being the Slayer?" Michael

countered, a half-smile tugging at his perfect lips.

"Yes. No. Most of the time. But not always," Buffy said, her words tumbling over one another. "Look, I didn't want to be called. It's screwed up my life in almost every way possible. But I helped a lot of people." She flashed for a minute on her high school prom, where her class thanked her for protecting them. "And so, I'm more okay with being the Slayer than not."

"And I'm okay with being what I am," Michael told her.

Buffy slammed her fists down on the table. "How can you compare yourself to me? Don't you get it?" She slowed her speech down, like she was talking to a small child. "Me—helpy. You—hurty."

"Only because you see the apocalypse as a bad thing," Michael answered.

"There's no other way to see it," Buffy cried.

"Do you know what the word 'apocalypse' means?" he asked. "It's Greek. It means a revelation of divine knowledge."

"I thought it meant misery, suffering, and devastation," Buffy said. "And that's what it looks like so far."

"We don't know what will come after this phase," Michael said. "The end of the earth doesn't mean the end of everything."

"So, what, something new will appear? Like a new planet? Or just new grass and everything?" Buffy sat up straighter. "'Cause that could be good. We've sort of messed up what we've got."

"I don't know," Michael answered. "I only know my piece of the puzzle."

"And you're willing to do your piece even if it seems evil?" Buffy asked.

"How do you define evil?" Michael countered.

Buffy opened her mouth to answer. She wasn't usually too big on philosophical conversations, but with Michael it was hard not to get engaged. Then it hit her: This was no philosophical exercise. She was sitting here having a nice, calm, rational conversation about the end of the world.

Anya appeared in the living room, making Spike jump. Ever since he'd seen the horrible monster, he'd been on edge. The others all thought he was crazy, but for the first time in months he actually felt sane. He knew what he'd seen.

Anya was breathing hard. "I've never trusted Buffy, and I want you all to know that I was right," she cried. "She's working with that demon! I saw the two of them sitting at the diner together."

"I'm sure Buffy was in the middle of a negotiation," Giles told her.

"Buffy was sitting with that nauseating, revolting . . ." Spike couldn't come up with the word. The thought of Buffy near that creature made him want to kill.

"Tell him how Michael really looks," Willow said from her place in front of the computer.

Spike tried to contain his anger. "Look," he said. "I

know that I've had a few . . . *spells* since I've come back but I know that thing is—"

"Repulsive!" Anya finished for him.

Giles jerked his head up from his note-taking. "What?" he exclaimed.

"I told you all I'm not bonkers," Spike said, shooting Anya a grateful look.

"No, Spike's right," Anya went on. "That demon is disgusting."

"Anya, please tell me exactly how he looked," Giles demanded. "This is very important."

"He had a mass of this horrible blond hair, and these awful blue eyes." Anya shivered. "Honestly, I could hardly stand to look at him."

"You ran when you saw him, didn't you? Admit it." Spike knew if he ran, Anya definitely ran.

"Of course I ran. I'm not crazy," Anya answered. "Well, I transported, anyway. Unlike your precious Buffy. She's sitting right there flirting with him." She shot a pointed glance at Xander.

"Enough, Anya," Giles scolded. "No one here doubts Buffy's loyalty." He paused for a moment, thinking, then turned to Willow. "Would you do a search for a being that appears beautiful to the good and hideous to the wicked?"

"Wicked? Who are you calling wicked?" Spike asked, although he already knew the answer.

"Just testing out a theory," Giles said.

"Anya, the git is calling you and me wicked," Spike went on. "Even though I have a soul, and I won't bore you with what I had to do to get it."

"Spike, all I'm saying is—," Giles started.

"Oh, I know what you're saying," Spike interrupted him. "Because we see that Michael thing as hideous and the rest of you lot think he's lovely, we're wicked and you're good."

"Well, you have killed several hundred people," Xander reminded him.

"When I had no soul," Spike shot back.

"Here's something," Willow said. "To the righteous he will appear as a beautiful star. To the wicked he will appear as a monster that rips their souls out of their bodies."

Everyone was silent for a moment. Even Spike had to admit that sounded pretty much on target. Giles sank down onto the couch, his face even paler than usual. "My god," he said. "Michael."

Willow shook her head. "That doesn't make sense. I saw Michael as beautiful. But if we're saying Michael is a being that the wicked should see as a monster, then I should see him as a monster. I've killed too. And I wanted to kill the whole world."

"That's different," Xander immediately said.

"Of course it's different," Spike shot back. "You have one set of rules for your friends, and one—"

"Hello? Can we focus?" Dawn snapped. "What kind of demon is that quote talking about?"

"I only found that snippet," Willow said. "There are no details. Giles?"

Giles roused himself and turned to face them. He looked ill. "I take it none of you went to Sunday school or the like?"

Anya let out a snort. "You can say that again," Xander agreed with her.

"Although I'm sure it will be hard for you to believe, I did have some religious education when I was a boy," Spike admitted. "Can't say I remember anything about stars and monsters."

"Just tell us, Giles," Willow pleaded.

"I'm afraid we're dealing with something—or rather, someone—rather unprecedented," he answered.

"Why? What kind of demon is he?" Willow asked.

"If I'm correct, he's not a demon. In fact, he's not in any way evil," Giles answered. "And that's the problem."

"Not in any way evil? What does that mean?" Dawn said.

"I believe our Michael is an angel," Giles answered.

Xander laughed. Then he took a look at Giles's serious face. "An *angel*?" he said. "There's no such thing."

Spike rolled his eyes. "And how about vampires, mate?" he asked. "Werewolves? Demons? They don't exist either, do they?"

"Okay, point taken," Xander said. "But an angel? That seems so . . . Christian."

"Actually, several religions have beings that could be considered angels," Willow put in. "Though I don't know why we would think Michael was one."

"It's a very specific description," Giles said tiredly. "The angel is seen as beautiful by the good and horrible by the wicked."

"No. You have it wrong," Anya announced. "I'm not wicked, so that thing isn't an angel or I wouldn't have seen him as ugly."

"Not wicked? *You?* How do you figure?" Spike scoffed.

"Because I help people, women people," Anya answered. "I grant their wishes." She faced Spike, her green eyes glowing with passion. "I *punish* the wicked! So how can I *be* the wicked?"

"You did choose to become a vengeance demon again," Giles gently reminded her.

"Well, what about me, then?" Spike demanded. "I'm not wicked. I have a soul. And this bloody chip in my head. I've killed nothing but demons for years now."

"It doesn't seem that having a soul automatically means you're righteous," Giles replied. "You are, technically, still a vampire. A demon."

"Who knows what I would have done with my soul if I'd had it all along?" Spike said, talking to himself as much as to anyone in the room. "I could have been a right bastard with the bloody thing."

"That's not the point," Anya said impatiently. "The point is why should that Michael thing be deciding what is wicked and what isn't? You want to know who I think is wicked? Xander Harris, that's who."

"Me?" Xander protested, his voice coming out in a half-squeak.

"Xander?" Spike shot a sideways glance at him. "He's too much of a milquetoast to qualify as wicked.

Annoying, that's as much as I'd give the boy."

"When he walked out on our wedding . . ." Spike could see the sheen of tears in Anya's eyes, and he slung his arm around her shoulders. He couldn't stand crying. "But no, he looked at it and saw the beautiful star. It's not fair."

"Anya—," Xander started.

"Don't," she ordered. Anya swiped furiously at her eyes, even though tears hadn't started to fall. "Starseer." She jerked her head toward Willow. "And what about her? She's right. She should have seen the thing as a monster. She's a killer. And she wrecked the Magic Box." Anya scrubbed at her eyes again. "And light bulb girl," she spat at Dawn. "If it's a soul thing, do you even have one? Giles, what about you? Are you saying you never did anything bad when you were Ripper? How'd you get that name, anyway?"

They all just stared at her, speechless. Spike slowly stepped away as Anya seemed to get herself under control again. She pulled a Twinkie out of the closest box and pasted a smile on her face.

"Okay, so what do you want me to do to fight this disgusting guy?" she asked. "If I'm not too wicked to help."

Have to love the girl, Spike thought. *She bounces back.*

Giles abruptly stood up and began to pace. "Well, Anya, I'm sure we all appreciate the offer," he said. "But I'm not sure there *is* a way to fight Michael."

Even Spike was surprised to hear Giles say something like that. "Why not?" he asked. "What does he want?"

"If I'm correct about Michael's real identity, he wants to bring about the apocalypse," Giles replied. "The *true* apocalypse."

CHAPTER SIX

Willow looked up as the front door banged open. Buffy dropped her weapons bag on the floor with a clatter and came into the living room.

"Good, you're all here," she said. "I had a little after-school conference with Michael, and the scoop is, he claims he's an angel. With a capital *A*." She looked around the room. "I was expecting some oohs and aahs," she said.

"We kind of got there too," Willow explained.

"Yeah," Xander bit out. "Giles was just explaining that because Michael is an angel it's pointless to try and stop him."

"What?" Buffy sank down on the sofa next to Willow. "We have to stop him. He says he's starting the apocalypse."

"Yes. Well. I'm afraid we have to consider the possibility that the true end of days is indeed what we are faced with," Giles admitted.

"I don't understand," Buffy said. Willow took her hand.

"I'm still stuck on the angel part," Xander told Giles. "I just don't believe in them."

"I assumed he was delusional," Buffy admitted. Dawn sat down on the arm of the sofa next to her and Buffy wrapped her arm around her sister.

Giles began to pace again. He'd been pacing pretty much since the word "angel" first came up. Willow wished he would stop. But she thought maybe it helped him keep it together, like he could sort of pretend that he was in a lecture hall and that this was all just theoretical. At least, as long as he was pacing and talking.

"Well, Xander, you may be thinking of angels as they are portrayed in popular culture—white-robed creatures with wings and the like," Giles said in his best disapproving-professor voice.

"Yeah. Or Irish chicks with long dark hair," Xander said.

"When in fact the pop culture angel evolved from the earlier Christian version of an angel, which came from the Hebrew angel, which in turn is an evolution of the ancient Zoroastrian idea of an angel," Giles said. "Or possibly the Hebrews got the idea from the Greeks. No one's really sure."

"What's the *z*-thing?" Dawn whispered to Willow.

"It's a really old religion, one of the oldest we know about," Willow whispered back.

"The point is, the concept of angels runs through almost all of the major religions of the world," Giles went on. "Judeo-Christian angels, Greek daimons, Arabic djinn, Gnostic genii . . . whatever you want to call them, they've always been there: superhuman creatures that act as messengers from the divine being. Or beings. The Powers That Be."

"I thought djinn were mischievous spirits," Willow said, trying to remember what she'd learned in her world beliefs class.

"Well, yes," Giles replied. "Not every religion believed that angels were inherently good. Just that they were there, between human and deity."

"So we have a bad angel," Xander said. "See, now *that* I can get on board with."

"I didn't say that, Xander," Giles snapped. Willow shot Buffy a worried look. She'd never seen Giles so on edge before.

"This concept of judgment . . . ," Giles said, his voice softening as he looked around the room at them. "The idea that this particular angel appears as one thing to the good and another to the wicked . . . It's . . . well, it's a prophecy of the end time. In some strains of Judaism, this would be the role of the messiah. In Buddhism, it's Metteyya who appears to the good, while the wicked cannot see him."

"But he *doesn't* appear different," Willow argued. "He looks the same to everyone. Anya, didn't you say you saw Michael with blond hair and blue eyes?"

"Yes," Anya said, shuddering. "He was horrible."

"See?" Willow said. "He looks the same. People just interpret him differently."

"Yeah, Anya and I have very different taste in men," Buffy agreed. "No offense, Xan."

Willow turned to Spike. "No!" she barked. She could tell by the look on his face that he'd been about to make a snide remark to Xander. Spike closed his mouth and looked away.

"I hope you're right," Giles said. "But from the ancient Persians to the modern Buddhists, all the major religions involve prophecies of the end times. This will be a time of judgment, during which people are prepared for paradisaical existence or eternal torments." Giles paused for breath. "In many of these religions it is said to be an angel that starts the apocalypse as the divine being's, er . . ."

"Hit man," Xander volunteered.

"Xander, don't," Willow burst out. She didn't know what she believed, at least not yet. But she didn't think it was right to compare something divine to Tony Soprano.

"Have you looked out the window, Will? All the trees and plants are dead," Xander shot back. "Do you think something nice did that?" He turned his attention to Giles. "I get that it's another apocalypse. What I don't get is why it matters whether an angel or a divine being or a Powerpuff Girl is involved. It's the apocalypse. We fight it. Discussion over."

Giles sank down on the sofa on the other side of Willow. She tentatively took his hand and he held on tight. "I don't think you're understanding," Giles said, and Willow could feel his fingers shaking.

No more Mr. Professor, she thought. *Just a scared normal person like the rest of us.*

"It's true, we've faced apocalyptic situations many times—"

"And kicked their asses," Buffy interrupted.

"And won," Giles agreed. "But I believe this is something different. Mind you, I'm only speculating. Still, just as our world had a beginning, it will have an end, an end that is natural and right."

Willow asked the question she didn't want to ask. "This is it, you think? This is the right time for the world to end?"

Giles started to stand up again. Willow knew he wanted to pace some more, but she refused to let go of his hand. She wanted him next to her.

"Possibly. A common thread in beliefs about the end of the world is that a series of events will occur as the world winds down," Giles explained. "What leads me to believe that the one true apocalypse may have begun is that we have already experienced several of them: the flood, famine, the raising of the dead. That's not a parlor trick that any old demon can do."

"Plus me and Buffy and Dawn and Xander seeing Michael as beautiful, and Spike and Anya thinking he was repulsive," Willow added. She didn't really want to help build the case for the end of the world having started, but she thought they should have all the facts laid out.

"So this is it," Xander said. "Game over." His voice was rough with sarcasm.

"There are circumstances to suggest so," Giles said. "And if, if this . . . *situation* does come to be, we might be well advised to see it not just as an end, but as a beginning. Every culture's beliefs about the end of world also speak of rebirth."

"The Aztecs thought the world had ended and begun again four or five times already," Anya put in.

Willow looked at her in surprise.

"What?" Anya said defensively. "I spent some time in South America in my early days as a demon. They were big into vengeance there."

"And so we do nothing? We just sit on our hands?" Xander asked. He scrubbed his forehead with his fingers, clearly struggling to comprehend this.

"Xander . . ." Willow didn't really know what to say. How could she comfort him when they were all feeling the same fear?

"I don't get it. What have we been doing all these years?" Xander cried out. "Why not just let the world go *pop* any of the last ten times we saved it? What was the point if it was all going to end anyway?"

Giles took off his glasses and looked at Xander steadily. "What's the point in living life to the fullest when we're all going to die anyway?"

Xander shook his head. "Not the same."

"I think it is," Giles answered.

"Are you saying if this Michael guy is the real deal there's nothing we can do to stop this? Nothing?" Xander asked.

Now we're just going in circles, Willow thought. It was time to break the tension crackling between Giles and Xander. "Hey, who's hungry?" she said. "I don't think we ever ate dinner. How about some Twinkie kabobs? Or, ooh, I could try and scoop out the filling and make soup!"

That sounded almost old-Willow, Willow thought. *And I wasn't even trying that hard.* Unfortunately no one took the bait. Giles and Xander were still glaring at each other, and everyone else looked confused. Willow nudged Buffy. "We have to do something," she whispered.

Slowly Buffy stood up. "Giles, is there any way we can confirm this?" she asked. "Whether or not Michael's really an angel and not just some demon with delusions of grandeur?"

Giles shook his head. "Demons and angels . . . they're different versions of the same thing, according to the most ancient beliefs. I don't think there's a litmus test to tell if he's the real thing or not."

"You talked to him, Buffy," Dawn said. "What did he say?"

"Who cares?" Xander put in. "He has that super-mojo that makes everyone love him no matter what he says."

"He turns it off when he's with me," Buffy said. "When I talked to him, I was thinking clearly. I know it."

"And?" Xander pressed.

Buffy glanced up at him apologetically. "And I wanted to believe him. I mean, I told myself he was crazy. And evil. And needed to be stopped. But truthfully? When he said he was an angel I believed him."

Xander threw up his hands in disgust. "Well, that's just great."

"I didn't say we weren't going to try to stop him," Buffy replied. "I just . . . I don't know how we're going to do that yet. I didn't make a dent in the force field with my flower of death."

"Well, I volunteer for anything that's going to put a hurt on that beast," Spike said.

"Like what?" Buffy demanded. "I can't even touch him. Nothing has worked."

"Did he say anything else?" Willow asked. "Like, did he tell you what's next? Or what the timetable is?"

"Yes," Buffy said. "He said we have two days left."

Dawn gasped. "Two days? That's it?"

"That's plenty of time," Xander said uncertainly. "What's the plan, Buff?"

"I don't know," Buffy said. She turned to Giles. "Can you check in with the Watchers Council? See if they know something about fighting the forces of good?"

Giles stood up. "Absolutely not," he said in a clipped tone.

"What?" cried Xander.

"What's wrong with you?" Spike added, stepping up to Giles as if he wanted to fight. This was getting out of hand.

"This is a matter of belief," Giles snapped. "Do you think the Watchers Council has some sort of magic mirror they can look in to tell them if it's a real angel or not?

How am I supposed to get to them, anyway? I doubt the phone lines are still up in the middle of the apocalypse."

"You won't even try!" Xander yelled.

"No, I will not," Giles yelled right back. "I was trained to fight the forces of evil. Not to do battle with others on my own side."

"I thought I was on your side," Xander accused him.

"Stop it!" Buffy shouted. Willow held her breath as silence descended over the room. "We're not getting anywhere by fighting about it," Buffy said quietly. "Let's take a break."

"What do you mean?" Willow whispered.

"I have to think," Buffy replied in a strained voice. "We have two days left. Let's all just take the night off from one another before things get uglier." She shot a warning look at Xander.

"Fine," he snapped. "But then tomorrow we make a plan, right?"

Buffy sighed. "Right. We regroup in the morning and . . . and I'll have a plan."

Giles pinched the bridge of his nose with two fingers. "I suggest you all begin to think about what's most important to you. Just in case."

"What's important to me is staying alive," Xander muttered. "I'll see you tomorrow." He slammed out the front door. For a moment nobody spoke. Then Giles headed upstairs, and Anya grabbed her bag and headed for the door, followed by Spike. Buffy went toward the kitchen, and Dawn up to her room.

Willow sat in the living room, reeling from her friends' anger. She'd never felt so alone in her life.

CHAPTER SEVEN

Spike sauntered away from Buffy's house. "What's most important to me?" he muttered, imitating Giles's posh accent.

Buffy, a little voice in his head answered instantly and with supreme confidence. He hated that little voice.

"You can't have her," he told himself aloud. The girl had him walking the streets, talking to himself. He'd welcome the apocalypse. This was worse than any hell that The Powers That Be or whatnot could devise.

At the end of the block Spike caught sight of a demon bouncing out of town. Seemed like the only things left were demons. All the humans had either left or were hiding in their houses like frightened rabbits. Spike focused on the demon. It was bouncing like a kangaroo, except it only had one foot—that, and from the torso up it looked like a smallish man with a large pelt of chest hair.

Why don't I kill it? he thought. *I'm wicked. That's been determined. And what is most important to the wicked? I'm thinkin' killing stuff is right up there.*

"I don't like the looks of you," Spike shouted. The kangaroo demon stopped hopping and turned toward Spike.

"I hate blonds," the demon answered. "I've been screwed over by blonds more times than you can count." Its eyes went orange.

Spike felt the familiar sensation of the skin on his face pulling together, his incisors sharpening. *Play time,* he thought as his vampire face took hold.

He rushed at the demon, aiming low. He wanted to see how the mouthy creature liked having its one foot knocked out from under it.

Bam! Somehow that one big, hairy foot had slammed into Spike's chin, throwing him up off the ground. He landed on his butt and saw exactly how the demon had managed the attack. It was standing on its hands, letting that massive foot do the fighting for it.

The demon rocked back and forth on its hands, giggling. Spike licked the blood off his lip, then shoved himself to his feet. Before he'd completely regained his balance, the foot came at him again, stretching the distance between Spike and the demon with ease, as if the muscles in the demon's leg were made with elastic.

Spike didn't bother trying to stand up this time. He spotted a kid's skate lying on the sidewalk and hurled it at the demon's head. When the foot moved to block it, Spike went for his next weapon: a garden hose with a heavy sprinkler head attached. *Nothing like fighting in the suburbs,* he thought as he whipped the hose through the air a couple of times.

The foot came shooting at him, but Spike had time to go for his real target. As the foot slammed into his ear, he cracked the hose like a bullwhip and sent the metal sprinkler into the demon's head. And the kangaroo man toppled.

The fun was pretty much over; it only took Spike a moment to use his body to pin the demon to the ground. Its neck muscles weren't at all elastic. They made a nice crack.

Buffy would have liked that hose lasso, Spike thought as he continued down the street.

Buffy. There she was again. In his head.

He needed another demon. He found four spotted buggy ones who were looking for crushing. Too easy. Little Dawnie could have handled them, made Buffy proud.

He found a yellowish one that looked like something someone sick had coughed up. Not too amusing, that. More squishy and time-consuming than anything else. Buffy probably would have loved to see him covered in that muck.

Then three vamps looking for a fight found him.

That was a bit of fun. Or it should have been, if he could have stopped thinking about how Buffy would have looked slaying alongside him.

Spike continued through town, thinking of his latest battle. His body was tingling as his new wounds closed up. *Wish Buffy was with me,* he thought. Not that he needed the help, but if the end was really coming, fighting side by side with Buffy one more time might be as close to heaven as he'd ever get.

Buffy.

He sat down on the curb and rested his head in his hands. He rubbed his scalp with his fingers. *She's under there, same as that chip. I'm never going to get her out of my head.*

Make that your bleedin' heart, the little voice corrected, so sure of itself. He hated that voice.

Willow picked up one of the special white candles she'd used in the levitation spell. It had been a long time since her room had anything related to magick in it.

Because she'd gone too far, too deep. She'd gotten lost.

She rolled between her fingers the chalk she used to draw magick circles, letting the dry, powdery scent fill her. The odor led her to a memory, the memory of one of the first spells she'd done with Tara.

It had been so weird to actually practice magick with another person, someone who was almost a stranger, Willow remembered. They'd both been shy with each other. But the power coursing back and forth between them had been sweet and strong. It knew no boundaries. And looking back, Willow realized those early spells gave her a taste of the intimacy she and Tara would share later in their relationship.

Willow twirled the chalk in her fingers. They'd used it in the coven in England too. She whispered a blessing on all who still lived there. They'd been fearful of her, yes, but they'd taken her in. And she'd discovered that she could make a connection with the entire earth that was as intimate as the connection she had shared with Tara. It was so powerful she'd almost lost all sense of herself as Willow, and yet gained a stronger sense of her place in the world than she'd ever had before.

Willow crumbled the chalk to dust in her fist. *Is magick still the most important thing to me?* she wondered. *Am I that close to being completely obsessed again?*

As if in answer, Willow found herself standing in the woods. Warren was strung up in front of her. And she felt no pity. No compassion. She felt fury so intense it turned her blood to fire. And she felt glee so powerful she could laugh without stopping for a hundred years.

Then she did it. She used her power to turn him inside out, loving the sound of his screams.

"A dream," Willow gasped. "It was just a dream. I lay down and fell asleep." She pulled the comforter over her without bothering to take off her clothes.

And she tried to ignore the intoxicating mix of fury and glee that was still racing through her body. If

Michael really was supposed to judge the good and the wicked, she had a feeling he'd made a mistake about her.

"Beer, beer, beer, beer, buckets, strainers, beer," Xander said, studying his cart. "What else does a party really need?" He popped open another beer, poured it through the strainer to collect the maggots, then drank the clean beer out of his beer bucket.

"Label maker!" he cried. "To label the strainers and buckets. Very unsanitary to mix." He stumbled over to the store's hardware aisle and found himself a label maker and a couple of rolls of red label tape.

"Better try it out," he told himself. He'd started talking to himself on about the forth beer and was trying to have fun with it. He'd never been this drunk before. He wasn't sure he liked it. But wasn't that what people did when they had no hope? When they gave up even trying? Didn't people just go get drunk?

Xander took another swig from the bucket. The beer tasted horrible, but he'd rather be drunk on bitter-tasting beer than sober and just sitting around waiting for the world to end. And that's all his friends seemed interested in doing. After Giles's doomsday pronouncement, everyone had just gone off by themselves. To think about what was important, he figured.

"I know what's important," he announced to the deserted supermarket. "What's important is putting up a fight so the world doesn't end before you've had a chance to make anything of yourself."

Xander winced. Had that sounded self-pitying? He

was afraid he was feeling a little too sorry for himself. He turned his attention back to being drunk. After a few tries he managed to get the label maker out of the thick plastic wrapping. It took more than a few tries to get the tape loaded. "Harris, you're a genius," he complimented himself when he'd done it.

Laboriously he twisted the dial on the machine, choosing each letter carefully. When he was finished, he clipped off the tape, peeled off the back, and stuck the tape onto the nearest shelf. He giggled as he read the message: "Rupert Giles is stoopid."

He used his cart for balance and got to his feet. "Late. Time to get this party started. You're all invited!" he called to the empty store as he wheeled his supplies toward the door.

It wasn't working. He didn't feel any better. He hadn't forgotten about the maybe-apocalypse that they maybe couldn't fight. "It's not fair," Xander said to the cash register. There was no cashier to talk to. "I want to fight. Come up with a plan and carry out the plan and get back to living my life. That's what we always do."

The cash register didn't answer him.

"But I'm not the power guy," Xander babbled on. "My opinion doesn't count because I'm not the Slayer or the Watcher or the vampire or the demon or the witch. Or the Key." He raised his bucket in a toast to the cash register. "Looks like I get to die because my so-called friends are all under the spell of some dumb angel."

He decided that no one was going to ask him to pay for his beer, so he wheeled the cart past the cash register and headed for the door. "They're all wrong," he called over his shoulder to the cash register. "You'll see."

Anya pushed her shopping cart down the sidewalk, trying to estimate how many dollars of merchandise she had accumulated. *I bet on eBay I could . . .* She didn't finish the thought. *No,* she decided. *I want it all for myself. Or maybe that horrible Michael creature—*

For a moment Anya felt a spurt of hope. But no, she realized, the good ones never wanted jewels or nice clothes or sex. No wonder he had no problem destroying the world. He had no appreciation for what it had to offer.

What now? she wondered, tapping her fingers on the handle of her cart. Cash? The banks were all deserted, and money was very nice. Except that she didn't need money for anything, because she'd already taken everything she wanted.

And nobody had even told her she looked pretty in her new outfit, which would have cost, if she'd had to use money, thousands and thousands of dollars. Not counting jewelry. It wasn't much fun dressing up if no one said you looked pretty and wished they could have all the fabulous things you had.

"Looting, are we?"

"Shopping," Anya corrected Spike, feeling ridiculously happy to see him. Maybe he'd tell her she looked pretty. It wouldn't count that much, because he wouldn't really be jealous and he'd have no idea how much her outfit cost, but it would be something.

"And you've been pining?" she asked.

"Brawling," he corrected her. "You'll see my conquests lying about all over town." He gave what he thought was a subtle muscle flex. *Poor deluded man,* Anya thought.

"It felt good to mix it up a bit," Spike continued. "Worked up a thirst." He hesitated. "Want to see if they have anything worth drinking over at the demon bar?"

"Well—" Anya cocked her head to the side, wanting to give the impression of thinking it over. "Shopping is very thirsty work."

Buffy picked up the mace—*spiked flail,* she corrected herself—and used newspaper to wipe off the top layer of mud. Then she began to polish the metal ball, careful not to miss a single one of the wicked points. Next she worked on the chain. Finally she treated the wooden handle with oil and gently replaced the flail in her leather weapons bag.

That was the last of them. Her babies were all clean and safe and stowed away where they belonged. Buffy picked up the bag, then set it down. She wasn't ready to leave the garage yet. She felt too restless.

Almost on autopilot, she began to stretch, then launched into one of her tai chi routines. From there she moved into shadow boxing. She worked until she was coated with sweat and her breath was coming hard. She worked until she felt ready for anything.

Even for killing an angel? she wondered. She couldn't face the idea of killing Michael. She'd wanted to hate him at first, but after talking to him—really talking—she couldn't shake her feeling of belief in him. Buffy sighed. She knew she'd disappointed Xander by not launching into action instantly. She knew the others felt at a loss without her leadership. She should be coming up with a plan to stop the apocalypse.

But how? She couldn't fight Michael. He'd proven that already many times. And more important, she didn't *want* to fight him. He was . . . nice. Even without putting his thrall on her, he'd impressed her. And what if he *was* an angel? Surely she wasn't supposed to go around trying to kill angels?

"I'll figure it out later," she muttered. "After I finish training."

But what was she training for? The world was ending.

Still, training gave her comfort. She wasn't some kind of commander who knew how to make decisions about things like angels and destiny. She was a soldier, just a simple fighter.

It comes down to this, no matter what, she thought. But was being the Slayer the most important thing to her?

The answer came easily. No.

Dawn stared at the sheet of lavender paper. All she'd written so far were the words "What's important to me."

This shouldn't be so hard, she thought. *There are all kinds of things I want.* "I want to talk to Todd Fisher," she wrote in a rush, just because the nearly blank paper was making her nuts. "I want to go to my prom. I want a McJob. I want to dye my hair red. I want to be a rock star. I want—"

Dawn balled up the paper and threw it across the room. All those "wants" were just wants. They weren't important. What *was* important?

Something thunked against Dawn's door, pulling her away from her thoughts. "Open up," Buffy called.

Dawn smiled. She leapt off the bed, reached the door in two steps, and flung it open. She laughed when she saw Buffy. Her sister was holding about twenty stuffed animals.

Buffy lurched into the room and dumped the animals on the bed. "Now, I know none of these is Mr. Happy," she told Dawn. "But I do have a very nice Mr. Gordo." She pulled a pink stuffed pig as round as a barrel out of the pile and handed him to Dawn. "I also have a Miss Whizzy, and, yes, I'm afraid she was some kind of toilet-training incentive." Buffy thrust a one-eared koala at Dawn. "Horsity-horse, no comments on the name, please, got me through the chicken pox. Excellent for squeezing." She tossed the yellow pony at Dawn.

"Okay, okay, you're forgiven!" Dawn exclaimed, hugging the animals to her chest. She felt her muscles relax, muscles she hadn't even realized were tense. "And you don't have to give me all of these. Just half."

"I'm sorry I didn't know how important Mr. Happy was to you," Buffy said. "I shouldn't have given him away. If ever you needed a Mr. Happy, it's now."

Dawn felt her throat get tight. "All I need is you," she answered. "But you're always off doing Slayer duty."

"Well, not today." Buffy wrapped her in a hug. "You got me, Dawn. Till the end."

Dawn closed her eyes and soaked in the love in her sister's embrace. Then she pulled back. "I know I do," she said. "But you shouldn't be here."

Buffy frowned in confusion.

"You need to talk to Michael," Dawn told her. "He's the one doing all these horrible things. He's the only one who can help us."

She looked Buffy right in the eye. "Giles is in his room. I won't be alone," she said. "Go."

Buffy went.

CHAPTER EIGHT

"No, I'm telling you, it really is the end time," the giant purple demon insisted, tears continuing to fall into his maggot-infested piña colada. "My mama told me stories about how it would be since I was six feet tall."

"It's not fair," Anya said. "At least demons should have a demon judge. A demon is the only one who can really say if another demon has been good or bad."

"Oh, shut it, both of you," Spike snapped. He'd listened to the one crying and the other complaining for the entire night. He'd have moved to better company, but they were the only two in the bar.

"Hey, here, have a napkin." Anya slid one that had been used, but just a little, toward the purple demon.

"Did your mama ever mention if bad humans and bad demons end up in the same place?"

The demon shook its head, hurling hot tears over the bar.

"All I wanted was a nice, quiet drink." Spike downed his shot of Jack Daniels, not bothering to fish out the maggots. Like worms in tequila, weren't they?

"I'm just having a little conversation," Anya protested. "I'm thinking maybe I could get Xander to do something really nasty." She rubbed her finger idly over one of the scorch marks the crybaby's tears had made in the wood of the bar.

"Or maybe I'm only a few points away from being on the nonwicked side," Anya chattered on. "I'm sure all those women I helped count for something." She leapt off her bar stool and hurried down to the other end of the bar. She studied the purple Barney wanna-be for a moment, then gave him two hearty pats on the back. "There, there," she said cheerfully. Then she trotted on over to Spike and planted herself back on her stool.

"Anya," Spike said, his patience worn as thin as a supermodel, "I went to Africa and fought a flame-fisted steroid eater, among other things, to get my soul back. And I'm still one of the wicked." He clutched his shot glass with both hands. "D'you really think patting a drunken demon crying in a bar is going to put you on the other team?"

"No." She frowned.

"Why do you want to be with Xander anyway?" he asked. "I thought you hated him."

"I do," Anya said. "But he's the only man I ever loved."

"I hear you, girl," said a soft voice from the doorway. Spike glanced up to see Clem.

"Thank god, someone sane," Spike said, pulling up a bar stool for the demon with the floppy folds of skin on his face.

"Oh, no thanks," Clem said. "I'm taking off. You two want to share a ride out of town?" he asked, glancing back and forth between them with his large, kind eyes.

"No thanks, mate," Spike answered. "We—"

"Did you see it?" Anya interrupted. "The Michael thing?"

Clem shuddered. "Worse than that thing I found on my deep sea fishing trip—*after* it exploded." His skin folds quivered as he glanced around, keeping an eye out for Michael. "I'm gonna boogie."

"You can't outrun it," Spike said. "Word is this is the real end. That thing is judging the good and the wicked."

"And it's going to send us to some kind of horrible hell dimension," Anya griped.

The purple demon made an anguished gurgling sound.

"Nah, I don't believe that," Clem said. "I bet it will just send us someplace where all the demons are together. You know, we'll think it's groovy even though the goody-goodys wouldn't like it."

"The way we all see the blond thing as disgusting and they fawn all over it?" Anya asked.

"But in reverse," Clem answered.

The purple demon heaved itself to its feet. "Can I have a ride?" it asked with a pathetic sniffle.

Clem's skin folds quivered. "Sure, Bobby," he said. "You two sure you want to stay?"

Spike nodded. "Don't let us keep you."

"Okay, then. Well, see you around." Clem gave Anya a moist, floppy hug. Spike stuck out his hand and managed to get away with a handshake.

Anya didn't bother to wait until Clem was out of earshot. "Now, if you were the big judge of everything, who would you say has done more bad things in his life—Clem or Xander?"

"Well, I suspect Clem cheats at cards," Spike said. "And he has questionable taste in television programs."

"But has he hurt anyone, really hurt anyone?" Anya exclaimed.

"We're men. We play poker. We have drinks. We don't talk," Spike protested.

"It's just wrong," Anya said decisively. She jumped off the bar stool and stomped toward the door.

"Now where are you going?" Spike asked. "Off to help little old ladies across the street?"

"I'm going to go make Xander have sex with me," Anya announced. "He hurt me. And I hate him. But if I'm never going to see him again, then we're having sex." She marched out of the door without another word.

That Anya, he had to hand it to her. She was a selfish little wench.

Anya popped her head back in the bar. "The

Michael creature seems to have put the sun out. If you felt like going anywhere." She slammed the door behind her.

Spike waited long enough to seem indifferent. Then he stood and walked out of the bar.

He couldn't hurl himself at Buffy. The thought repulsed him, reminding him of that other time. But he could look at her. He wanted Buffy to be the last thing he saw.

Xander's door was wide open when Willow showed up with the breakfast Twinkies. She stepped inside and followed the snoring. Xander lay on the living-room floor with his head half inside a bright red bucket. The whole place smelled like beer.

"Huh," Willow said. She started toward her clearly inebriated friend, wrinkling her nose when she spotted a strainer full of maggots. "Oh, Xan, what have you been doing?" she asked as she gently slid the bucket off his head. It was completely out of character for him to get drunk by himself. Or to get drunk, period.

I guess this end-of-the-world thing has us all behaving strangely, she thought.

Xander gave an extra-loud snore, but he didn't wake up. She decided to give him a little sleep-it-off time and sat down on the couch, which had some unopened beer cans strewn across it.

Nothing to read around here, Willow observed. She should tell Xander that books could be chick magnets too. That is, if there were more than two days to help him attract his businesswomen.

There will be, she told herself. *Buffy will come up with a plan. Giles will find out Michael's really a delusional demon. Something will happen to save us.*

Willow sat her purse on the coffee table next to Xander's toolbox and realized the metal box now had a red label on it: "Apacabox Memories." Cautiously she opened the box. She smiled when she saw the report on Sweden she and Xander had done together in the third grade. They'd used yellow yarn for the braids of the Swedish girl they'd drawn on the front cover. They'd both been very proud of it.

She set the report aside and found a note written on a scrap of paper: "Xan, can I borrow algebra notes? xxoo Buffy." Willow thought back to the supercrush Xander had had on Buffy when she'd first moved to Sunnydale, a crush so big he'd saved a note that had clearly meant nothing to Buffy. Willow smiled. She had a few notes like this from Xander to *her* tucked away, notes she was sure he wouldn't even remember writing.

Under the note were photos from three of Buffy's disastrous birthday parties. *Definitely taken pre-disaster,* Willow decided. *We all look so happy.*

They'd had a lot of good times, amazing times, even though those times were squeezed in between fighting evilness. Or maybe because of it.

Willow flipped to the next picture. Her and Tara. Arms around each other. Grinning into the camera. Willow stared at it, wishing she could crawl right in there, into her skin, and stay there safe in that moment with Tara forever.

Self-pity is so unattractive, she told herself. She dropped all the photos back in the box, replaced the Sweden report, and let the lid fall closed with a clank.

"Will, you came to my party," Xander slurred. He sat up and squinted at her. "Welcome. Wait. I got you your own bucket and strainer. They have your name on them."

"That's okay. I didn't come for the party," Willow said, with a horrified glance at the maggot-filled strainer on the floor.

"You didn't?" Xander asked. "Why?"

"You didn't invite me, for starters," Willow said.

"Oh. I knew I forgot something." Xander stumbled to his feet. "Excuse me for a second."

He disappeared into the bathroom. When he returned his face was wet and he seemed slightly more sober. "Sorry, I was still half asleep before."

Willow just nodded.

He sat down next to her and plucked a beer can off the couch. "I guess it wasn't all entirely a dream."

Willow shook her head, trying to look sympathetic.

"Did you see my—" Xander tapped the red label on his toolbox. "That's supposed to say 'Apocalypse Memories.'"

"Getting a little ahead of yourself, aren't you?" Willow asked.

"I was thinking about what Giles said, about what's important." Xander wrapped his arm around her and pulled her close in a half-hug. "It's you. It's my friends. I wanted something to show that. Something to leave behind. In case."

Willow hugged him back. "Xander," she said. "Are you okay?"

He pulled away from her a little. "Why shouldn't I be?"

"Well, 'cause you got all drunk, which you never do," she pointed out. "And, you know, 'cause the world is ending."

Xander jumped to his feet, then grabbed his head and sat back down. "It's only ending because we're letting it end," he muttered through gritted teeth.

Willow had expected him to say something like that. She knew he hadn't accepted the possibility that Michael was here to start the real apocalypse. She wasn't sure that she'd accepted it either. It just seemed easier to think the whole situation was out of their hands. Otherwise she might have to step up and use her magick. An unthinkable amount of magick.

"I saw the picture you put in of me and Tara," she said softly. "Thanks for that."

"Sometime, not in two days or anything, I think you'll be together," Xander said. "You two had the big It. True love."

Willow felt as if someone had reached into her chest and given her heart a hard twist. "I hope so. But . . . With the things I've done . . . Tara was such a good person. Genuinely kind. I don't think she ever intentionally hurt anyone, any nondemon anyone."

"Hey, when you looked at Michael, you saw cute, right?" Xander demanded. "That means you're a righteous chick."

"I thought you didn't believe he was an angel,"

Willow said. Because how could it be true that she was . . . righteous?

"So what? I don't care if he's the worst the Hell-mouth can spew. There's something in him that is a tester of good and evil. Evidence: Spike ran away from him. Demons are leaving town because he's here. Buffy melts when she's near him. You and Dawn both got swoony."

"I don't know what's true about heaven or hell or judgment or any of that," Willow answered. "I just don't feel like I deserve to be where Tara is."

"Okay, you want me to open the box, I'll open the box." Xander flipped open the lid of his Apocalypse Memories chest. He flipped through quickly and pulled out a picture of Buffy. "Okay, brought her back from the dead."

"Buffy didn't even want—," Willow began.

"Ask Buffy now if she wants to be here," Xander said. "I think she'll tell you yes. And mean it."

He waved the Buffy picture in her face. "Besides, you brought her back that other time, when she was afraid to come out of her head. If you hadn't gotten her back, Glory would have creamed us. And the world would have ended. So, there you go, you saved the world."

"It wasn't just me—," Willow began.

"Buffy would not have been there if you hadn't pulled her out of her little mental hideout; hence, you saved the world." Xander shook his finger at her. "No arguments, missy."

It was so hard to accept, to take it in, to see herself as Xander saw her. But Willow tried.

"And I'm not even done with this one picture," Xander said. "Note the cross that Buffy is wearing. The cross given to her by one Angel—damn, it would sound so much better if I had a last name here. What is it with these creatures and their no last names?" Xander shook his head. "Doesn't matter. My point—you gave Angel his soul back."

One of her first big uses of magick. It had worked a little too late, but still, it felt so satisfying. So right.

"And Angel, not that I'm the president of his fan club or anything, has done a lot of good in the world with that soul you returned to him," Xander continued. "Every week he's helping someone or other with that detective agency. And I think you, my friend, deserve a percentage of that karma or whatever you want to call it."

Xander reached into the box. "Moving on."

Willow grabbed his hand. "I get your point."

"Well, let me spell it out for you anyway," Xander said. "You, Willow Rosenberg, are a powerful force of good."

"Maybe not so powerful anymore. I'm the one who messed up a basic levitation spell the other day," she reminded him.

"So we'll do it again today, before the big Plan B, or Plan C, or whatever plan we're on, meeting," Xander told her. "And this time you'll get it right."

"Great, you got our booth," Buffy said as she slid into the seat across from Michael. "And you had them blot out the sun. Very romantic."

"I thought you'd be spending time with Dawn and your friends," Michael said.

"Well, Dawn wanted me to come here and ask you how to stop the apocalypse," Buffy told him.

He smiled. "She's very direct."

"Yeah. So are you gonna tell me?" Buffy asked.

"It can't be stopped."

"Why not?" Buffy asked. "How does it work?"

"I get a sign and I awaken," Michael told her. "Then I begin my work."

"How?" she asked.

"Why does it matter?" Michael countered.

"Because you may think it's unstoppable, but I've fought a lot of unstoppable things," Buffy said. "Maybe there's a loophole."

"There's no loophole," Michael said. "You've never fought anything like this."

"Humor me," Buffy replied. "How are you doing all this stuff? The weather, and the plants, and the zombies?"

Michael just looked at her as if he wasn't sure he was allowed to tell her.

"Come on," Buffy coaxed. "When you made that sea monster, you threw a flowerpot in the water first."

"A bowl," he corrected.

Got him! Buffy raised her eyebrows and waited for him to continue.

Michael smiled, knowing she'd engaged him. "It's a clay bowl. There are thirteen of them."

"Do they all make sea monsters?" Buffy asked. "Because, you remember, I'm good with sea monsters."

"No." Michael hesitated, not meeting her eye.

"Oh," Buffy said, beginning to understand. "Each one is a bowl, right? A bowl for the hail, and one for killing the plants, and one for the snow . . ."

"Each contains an event," Michael said. "When the bowl breaks, the event is unleashed upon the world."

"And?"

"And when all thirteen are broken, it will be over."

Buffy's head spun. She'd dealt with a lot of strange and powerful things in her years as the Slayer, but she'd never heard of this kind of magick before. "I'm guessing you didn't get those bowls at Pottery Barn," she said. "Do you make them?"

"No. They're each different. And it's almost as if they are made of part of the event itself. The one for the blizzards was crystalline, and you saw the one for the sea creature—it looked almost like a shell. They're beautiful."

He sees beauty in everything, even destruction, she thought. "So where do they come from?"

"They come to me when I need them," Michael said. "When it's time, they appear in my hands."

"But that's easy," Buffy told him. "The event doesn't happen until you break the bowl, right? So you can just stop breaking the bowls. It's not like some kind of earthquake or plague or something is gonna leak out of the bowl if you don't break it. Right?"

He stared at her as if she'd gone crazy. "I must break the bowls," he said.

"Why?" Buffy asked.

"Because it's my job," he replied. "It's my entire reason for being."

"But no one is making you do it, are they?" she pressed. "You're the one who actually breaks them."

"Well, yes." Michael still looked baffled. "But I have no choice."

"Of course you do," Buffy answered. She leaned across the table toward Michael. "You have to stop. You're in the process of slaughtering millions of innocent people. How about if my friend Xander makes you a nice cabinet to keep the bowls in. Something really sturdy. Yet attractive."

Michael sighed. "Remember what we talked about? You were called to be the Slayer. I was called to do this."

"Here's the thing," she told him. "If some old British guy had showed up and said, 'Hey, you're the Chosen One. The first thing you must do is kill all the puppies in town,' I wouldn't have done it."

Buffy tucked her feet underneath her on the bench. Even arguing with Michael, she couldn't help feeling comfortable around him. It wasn't the warm, gooey feeling she'd originally gotten from him. It was just genuine . . . respect. They disagreed, but she still got the feeling he was a force of good.

"Even when I knew I was the warrior of the people," she went on, "and that a lot of people would die if I didn't step up, I didn't just say, 'Where do I sign?' I had a lot of questions. A lot of complaints. A lot of general whines. Did you ever whine, Michael? Did you ever ask one question?"

"I don't have a choice. The sign comes. I awaken. I fulfill my destiny," Michael answered.

"When you say you have no choice, what does that mean exactly?" Buffy asked. Usually she found herself avoiding the intensity of Michael's gaze, but this time she locked eyes with him. "Do you mean it's physically impossible for you not to break the next bowl? Are you controlled somehow?"

"No." Michael smiled. "Buffy, I am much older than you are. It's true, I have been asleep since time began. But not completely unaware. I have felt many beginnings. And many endings. They don't frighten me the way they do you."

Buffy sighed in frustration. "I'm just trying to understand." And she was getting nowhere. "Can you tell me what happens next? What's going to come out of the next bowl? Where will you be when it appears in your hands?"

Michael shook his head. "I don't know what will be inside the bowl until I open it. I know there are two days left. But I don't know when or where the bowls will appear to me."

"So you have no idea why you started this whole thing in my town," Buffy said.

"No, but I'm glad I did. I wanted to meet you, Buffy."

Buffy tried to think of something else she could ask him, anything that might help. "Okay, what about the sign you were talking about? The one that woke you up? What's the deal with that?"

"I was waiting for the arrival of a wolf in sheep's

clothing," he explained. "It came." He stretched his arms out wide. "And here I am."

Buffy took that in. A wolf in sheep's clothing? A literal wolf in sheep's clothing? "I saw that sheep-wolf. I killed it in about three minutes," she exclaimed. "How could it have been so important?"

"It was the sign. That's all I can tell you, because that's all I know. But that's enough for me." Michael stood up. "I have to go."

"Got a volcano to set off?" Buffy asked.

"Something like that."

CHAPTER NINE

"Okay, Will, let's get busy," Xander said, pushing open the door of Willow's bedroom. He was doing his best to concentrate on his best friend's problem. It helped keep his mind off other things, like, say, the impending apocalypse. He had taken a shower, drunk as much maggot-strained water as he could choke down, and devoured three aspirin. His hangover was a thing of the past. He felt like a new man.

Willow, on the other hand, looked like crap. She sat on her bed, staring silently at him. Her skin was even paler than usual, and sweat beaded her furrowed brow. For a moment he wondered if she was about to get sick. "Did you eat a maggot by mistake?" he asked.

She shook her head, looking a little sicker at the

thought. "I'm just nervous," she mumbled.

Xander couldn't help feeling surprised. "But there's nothing to be scared of," he pointed out. "Pretty-boy Michael's doing a good job of starting the apocalypse. If we screw up again, we'll just blame it on him."

Willow shrugged. "I never said it was a rational fear," she replied. Her big eyes met his imploringly. "We don't have to do this. It's kinda pointless now, anyway."

"I think there might be more point to it than ever," Xander said. "I'm a 'the only good apocalypse is a dead apocalypse' kind of guy. And I think you can help with that."

"But if Giles is right, there's nothing we can do," Willow reminded Xander. "And we don't know Buffy's plan yet."

Xander felt a spark of anger, then realized what Willow was doing. "You're playing me. You know it, and I know it. You've been doing it since kindergarten. 'Oh, Xander, why do we have to finish our coloring? The apocalypse is starting tomorrow,'" he whined in a high voice.

Xander crossed his arms over his chest. "We're doing it. The *point,* besides the somewhat obvious one, is to get you over your greatest fear. Because otherwise you're going to die with regrets."

Then his own words caught up with him. "Did I just say die?" He began to hyperventilate. He sat down quickly next to Willow.

"I know," she said in response to his unspoken freak-out. "You'd think we'd be used to it by now, the whole this-may-be-our-last-day-on-earth thing."

"Yeah," he agreed. "But it gets me every time."

They sat in companionable silence for a moment. Xander realized that his mind had gone completely blank. Well, not blank so much as numb. Usually when there was a major supernatural crisis he had lots to occupy his thoughts—like how to kill a demon or outsmart a government conspiracy. Where to hide, how to get to Buffy as fast as possible for protection. That sort of thing. Whatever the crisis, there was always some kind of plan, and he always had some little assignment to help carry out the plan. But this waiting was killing him. *That's because I'm waiting to die,* he realized.

He stood up so suddenly that Willow fell sideways from the shock wave to the mattress. "We're doing the levitation spell," he announced. "You need to get over your fear of magick. And I need to be in denial. Let's go."

Reluctantly Willow got off the bed. She pulled a thin notebook from her desk and tossed it onto the ground. Then she arranged the three white candles. He watched as she used white chalk to begin making a magick circle on the floor. "Wasn't there something else?" he asked, trying to remember how they'd done this spell last week.

"The pot on the shelf," Willow said, continuing the circle.

Xander glanced over at her bookshelf and noticed the small glass pot full of brownish-yellow gunk. He wrinkled his nose. No wonder he'd forgotten about it. That stuff reeked. He'd probably blocked it out after last time. But if they needed it for the spell, then he would just have to suck it up and smell the grossness. *It's for Willow,* he reminded himself, reaching for the pot.

He set it down next to the notebook. Willow had just completed the circle. She plopped down cross-legged on the floor inside of it. Xander did the same.

"So do we want to do everything we did last time?" he asked. "Or are we trying to change something? You know, to make sure the spell actually levitates something instead of just shooting lightning bolts out the window again."

"Power," Willow corrected him. "Concentrated magick power, not a lightning bolt."

"You say tomayta, I say tomahta," Xander replied. "How do we keep it from happening?"

Willow chewed on her lip, thinking about it. "I still don't know for sure what went wrong," she said slowly. "I mean, the power shot out the window because you knocked my hand"—she shot him an exasperated look just like the old, unafraid Willow would have—"but we didn't find any signs of a levitation. So I have to assume that the spell didn't work at all."

"Then why the power bolt?" Xander asked.

"I'm not sure," Willow admitted. She began to look worried again.

"I think we probably did it right," Xander said quickly. "Just because we didn't *find* anything levitating doesn't mean we didn't *make* anything levitate. For all we know, our power shot out the window, picked up a gnat, and levitated the heck out of it. We wouldn't have noticed that."

Willow raised her eyebrows. "Gnats can fly," she said.

"See? I bet the gnat didn't even realize it was levitating," he replied. "It probably just thought it had lost weight or something. . . ."

"But I guess the only way we can be sure is to do everything the same way," Willow went on. "Except we'll be careful not to move our hands. That way the power will stay right here, whether it levitates anything or not. And then we'll see if the spell worked."

"Gotcha," Xander said. "No wild hand gestures."

Willow lit the three candles one by one in a line from right to left.

Xander picked up the pot of brown gunk. "Last time I spread this on the notebook. Do that again?"

Willow nodded. Xander scooped out some foul-smelling brownness and smeared it onto the cover of the book. He wiped his hand on his jeans. Willow watched nervously. Xander could see how frightened she was, so he put on his warmest smile and held out his hands. "It'll be okay, Will," he said confidently. "I'm here. Nothing can go wrong when we're together."

She nodded, unconvinced. Then she took his hands. "Don't let go," she warned him. "Once I start the spell, we have to stay connected or it won't work."

"Got it," Xander said. He held on as she shifted her gaze down to the notebook. Willow opened her mouth to begin the spell, then hesitated. Her grip on his hands had tightened until it kinda hurt, but Xander didn't say anything. He just gripped her back and concentrated on sending positive energy her way. He wasn't sure exactly how to do that, but he figured that if she needed him, she'd take energy from him in some magickal fashion. For now, he just held on tight and kept his eyes on her face.

Willow moistened her lips and began again. "In the world, we are blind. In the candlelight, we see."

Her voice shook as she spoke, but she didn't falter. The spell came out just as he remembered it from last time. And now he found himself remembering exactly what had happened last time: There had been a fly buzzing around the notebook throughout the entire spell. As Willow had finished the fly tried to dive-bomb Xander's left eye, so he'd automatically reached up to swat it away. He'd dropped Willow's hand, and the burst of power had shot from her fingertips and out the window.

Just thinking about it made Xander want to move his hand. As Willow spoke he thought about the fly, thought about wanting to swat it. He felt itchy, as if flies were crawling all over him. *Must move my hand,* he thought. It was the one thing he couldn't do. It was the only thing he wanted to do. . . .

"In the world, we lie still. In the circle, we fly," Willow finished.

I did it! Xander thought. He'd made it through the spell without moving his hand! He grinned at Willow. Her eyes had gone a little bit black, but otherwise she was normal Willow. She smiled back. Then a blinding flash of light filled the room, accompanied by a loud shrieking sound. Xander fell backward, Willow's hands slipping out of his grasp.

For a moment he couldn't see. He was blinded by the power burst.

Then he heard a strange sound. A low, throaty growl coming from right in front of him. That couldn't be Willow, could it? Even when she'd been trying to destroy the world, she hadn't *growled*.

The blindness lasted no more than a second. Soon there were black spots swimming in front of Xander's eyes. He blinked rapidly, trying to clear them, and finally looked with perfect vision right into the eyes of the wolf.

"Whaaaa!" Xander yelped, scrambling to his feet.

In the center of their magick circle sat a snarling, long-fanged, yellow-eyed, not-very-happy silver wolf. And he sure wasn't levitating.

Buffy scuffed her heels along the pavement as she walked down the sidewalk. She didn't enjoy the sound of the concrete against her shoe, but at least it was normal. The sidewalk was just the same as ever, and so was the annoying sound that resulted from scraping your foot against it. Nothing else was the same. It had gone from snowing to scorching heat to below-zero temperatures again all in this one morning. She glanced up as she reached her yard. The grass was dead. Just thin little strips of crispy brown lying flat against the dirt. The flowers her mom had planted near the front bushes had all shriveled into nothing, and even the giant old oak tree on the lawn was nothing more than a rotting trunk with no leaves.

I'm glad Mom isn't here to see this, she thought. Although, for selfish reasons, she did wish her mother was here. Buffy wanted a hug, a hug from the one person in the entire world who had ever been able to make her believe that things might be okay eventually. Instead, it was she herself who would have to be there for everyone else, especially after she told them what she'd learned from Michael. That no plan in the world was going to stop this apocalypse.

Then she'd have to be strong. For Dawn . . . and Spike.

Buffy stopped walking just to see what Spike would do. He'd been following her ever since she left the diner. He was trying to be stealthy, but the truth was that he'd kinda lost his touch ever since he got his soul back. Not that he wasn't still a vampire, it was just that he'd lost some of his edge—his well-honed vampiric skills had slipped. He couldn't do that whole moving-silently-like-a-cat thing anymore. Buffy figured that Spike just wasn't concentrating. It must be confusing to suddenly have all the demands of a soul on top of all the bloodlust demands of vampirism. Spike certainly *seemed* confused lately.

She stayed where she was, at the junction of the sidewalk and the walkway to her house. Spike stayed where he was, crouched behind the rusty remains of an abandoned Miata that barely hid him at all. How long should she give him? If he didn't come out on his own, should she go over and get him? Buffy sighed. She had no idea anymore what to think of Spike. She'd never loved him, she was pretty sure of that. But now he'd gone and gotten a soul—because of *her*—and she had to admit, she was touched. There was a certain satisfaction in knowing that she'd inspired a monster to try to reform. And no matter how she felt about him, she knew for sure that *he* loved *her*. Didn't that mean she had an obligation to be nice to him? She'd treated him badly while they were together. Didn't she owe it to him to at least make sure that he wasn't alone for the end of the world?

But then why was he making it so difficult? Why was he just following her around instead of coming straight to the point and actually talking to her? Buffy headed up the walkway toward the house. If he didn't want to come out from his hiding spot and face her, he could just stay out there. But the guilt hit her before she even reached the front door. She knew the answer to her own questions: Spike was staying away from her because he thought it was what she wanted, and he was following her because he just couldn't bear the thought of not seeing as much of her as he could before the end.

She pushed open the door and stopped. What kind of person would she be if she left him out here in the freezing, barren almost-apocalypse? He loved her. She should at least invite him in.

"Spike!" she called without turning around.

There was no answer.

"I know you're behind that car," she added. "Come inside."

Still no answer. But the rusty car gave a loud creak

as if someone had just leaned against it. She heard a faint whisper of "Bugger!"

Buffy couldn't help but smile. Poor Spike. He couldn't even hide properly anymore—the car had just given him away. She waited. Spike stayed where he was.

"Fine," she muttered. "I tried. Last chance!" she added, raising her voice so Spike could hear her.

"Oh, all right," he grumbled, unfolding his lanky frame from behind the hunk of metal. "Getting bloody uncomfortable anyway."

Spike ambled up the walkway toward Buffy, not meeting her eyes. "What, you're shy now?" she asked.

He shrugged. "It seems a little more real these days, the whole good and evil issue. I thought you'd want to keep away from evil. I might taint you."

"You mean because of what's going on?" she asked.

"Well, yeah," Spike said. "Your boy Michael is *judging* people. The good get one thing, the wicked get another. No middle ground."

Buffy considered that. "Did you think there was a middle ground?" she asked.

For the first time, Spike met her eye. "I thought good people were simps," he said. "Until I met you. You showed me that good has strength too. And hidden layers. So yeah, after that I thought there were some shades of gray."

Buffy's breath caught in her throat. Spike could always get to her somehow. He wasn't afraid to tell her exactly how he felt about her, and sometimes his honesty was like a slap in the face. She knew he'd done awful things throughout his long life. But somehow she'd always suspected there was good in him somewhere. She'd believed in a middle ground too. All this talk of Michael's about the wicked and the good made her uncomfortable. Deep down, she didn't feel entirely good. She felt like a warrior on the good side who'd privately done some bad, bad things. And Spike was the physical reminder of those things.

"Come inside," she said gently, reaching for his hand, finally willing to touch him. "We all need to talk."

She turned back to the house just as a scream came from upstairs. "What was that?" Buffy asked, instantly filled with adrenaline.

"Xander, I think," Spike replied, his face grim.

Buffy ran inside, heading straight for the stairs. But she hadn't gotten more than two steps up before she saw the wolf. The giant, yellow-eyed beast was charging right at her! She grabbed a stake from her jacket's inside pocket and prepared to do battle. The wolf showed no signs of backing down. Its predatory stare focused on Buffy and it snarled, revealing gleaming fangs dripping with saliva.

"Baaaa," the wolf growled.

Buffy stopped, shocked. The wolf kept coming, but its progress down the stairs slowed as the pads of its giant paws fused together, becoming dainty black hooves. The thick silver fur of the wolf's back was falling off everywhere, leaving behind tightly coiled brownish wool. It snarled again as it reached Buffy, but now its fangs were flat, grass-eating teeth. Buffy looked into the furious yellow eyes as they turned brown, their expression calming into docile indifference. "Baaa," the lamb said conversationally as it trotted past Buffy and down the last few steps. It gave Spike a wide berth and made its way out the door and down the walkway. Buffy let it go.

"What the bloody hell was that?" Spike sputtered.

Buffy realized her mouth was hanging open, and closed it. She watched the lamb turn onto the sidewalk and vanish with a wag of its tiny tail. "That was a wolf in sheep's clothing," she said.

"Well, obviously," Spike replied, rolling his eyes. "But what was it doing in your house?"

"I don't know," Buffy said grimly. "But I'm going to find out."

CHAPTER TEN

"**E**veryone in the living room. Now!" Buffy bellowed. A wild hope was trying to push its way into her mind, but she couldn't allow herself to get excited yet. She needed facts.

Willow and Xander came charging down the stairs, faces pale. "Buffy!" Willow cried. "Thank god you're home!"

"Did you kill the wolf?" Xander asked, looking around wildly.

"No," Buffy said shortly.

Xander's mouth dropped open. "Why not?"

Buffy stared at him. Why hadn't she killed it? Was she supposed to? She was too confused to answer. Luckily Spike saved her the trouble. "Because it's an important sign that needs to be investigated," he told Xander. "Don't you know anything?"

"Where's Dawn?" Buffy asked.

"Out taking a walk around what's left of the neighborhood with Giles and Anya, according to this," Willow said, waving the piece of paper she'd picked up from the coffee table. "Why? What's going on?"

"I need to know where that wolf came from," Buffy said. "I heard Xander scream, and then a wolf came running from upstairs."

Xander's cheeks reddened. "Well, it surprised me," he said, defending himself. "It was supposed to be a floating notebook."

"Why is it important, Buffy?" Willow asked.

"Because it turned into a sheep on the way downstairs," Buffy replied. "It was a wolf in sheep's clothing."

Understanding filled Willow's eyes. "Like that sheep you killed the other day," she said. "Only, you know, in reverse."

"Where did it come from?" Buffy pressed. She wished Giles were here. The whole signs thing was so Giles's area of expertise.

"We did a spell," Willow replied. "I mean, not a make-a-wolf spell . . . although I guess technically it *was* a make-a-wolf spell, since it made a wolf. But not on purpose. It was an accidental wolf."

Usually Buffy had no problem processing Willowspeak. But right now her brain was so full of hopeful possibilities that she had no room left over for translating. "Huh?" she said.

"We did a levitation spell to lift a notebook," Xander explained. "But the notebook didn't levitate. Instead, a wolf appeared out of thin air."

"And then did a little transformation on its way out to play," Spike put in.

"Was there a wolf in the house?" Anya demanded.

Buffy turned to see Dawn, Anya, and Giles at the front door. "Get in here!" she cried. "I think we may be on to something! Remember that wolf-sheep thingy I killed last week? We just saw another one."

"I think we just *made* another one," Willow put in. "My magick is all screwy. Xander and I wanted to levitate a book, not make a whole dog-type thing."

"*You* were doing a spell with *her*?" Anya demanded.

"It's our magick desensitization program," Xander explained. Anya had plopped herself down on the couch next to him and was trying to kiss his neck, but Xander kept talking. "Willow's afraid to use magick, so I figured we'd ease her back into it a little at a time. You know, start small and work up to the big stuff as she gets more comfortable."

"Sounds like a good plan," Dawn said.

"Who cares?" Anya grumbled, pulling Xander's arm around her. "The world is ending. She never needs to do magick again."

"Buffy might have a plan to stop it," Dawn added. "She went to talk to Michael again." Anya ignored her.

"No matter what, I just wanted to try one more time," Willow told them. "But I think I've lost my touch since I came back. I can't even get the simplest spell right. This time we made a wolf, last time we just shot the power out the window—"

"Hey, that was my fault," Xander put in, trying his best to escape from Anya's embrace. "I pulled my hand away and knocked your arm. Don't go blaming yourself for that one."

Sometimes Buffy wished her friends had a less rapid-fire way of talking. Like now, for instance. "Last time?" she asked.

"But we never found any evidence of the spell even working," Willow argued. "So for all we know, I did screw up and your knocking my hand didn't matter at all."

"What last time?" Buffy asked, raising her voice.

"I still think the evidence was inconclusive," Xander said.

"Hello?" Buffy yelled. "What are you talking about? What last time?"

"On Monday," Willow said, looking at her askance. "We tried the levitation spell on Monday and it didn't work, and then today we tried it again. And it didn't work again."

"It *did* work," Buffy said. "It made a wolf in sheep's clothing."

"You two made the sign?" Giles exclaimed, staring at Willow and Xander.

"Michael said it was the sign!" Buffy cried. Thank god Giles was here. He could help her make sense out of all this. "He said it was the sign that woke him up!"

"Well, sure, but the notebook stayed flat on the ground," Xander replied.

"It made the wolf in sheep's clothing on Monday, too," Buffy said. "That's the night I ran into it by the fountain."

"That's true," Willow said, surprised.

"You mean we shot the power out the window and the wolf appeared out there?" Xander asked. "Cool."

"Monday, the day you first saw Michael?" Giles asked Buffy.

"Right," Buffy answered.

"Kiss me," Anya commanded. Distracted, Xander did as he was told.

"No wonder we didn't find anything levitating outside," Willow said.

Buffy's thoughts were racing. The unnamed hope inside her had swelled until it filled all her senses. "They did it, didn't they?" she asked, grabbing Giles's arm.

"I believe they did," he answered, his voice filled with a mix of horror and awe.

"Did what?" Xander asked.

"Michael said he was awakened by a sign," she explained. "The thing that signaled him to start the apocalypse. And the sign was a wolf in sheep's clothing." She looked up at her two best friends. "You guys, *you* started the apocalypse."

"I can't believe I could do something so stupid," Willow muttered, flipping through one of the three magick books Giles had brought with him from England. She was talking more to herself than anyone else. And no one else seemed inclined to listen. Xander was busy trying to fight Anya off on the couch. Buffy and Spike had disappeared the instant Buffy realized that the apocalypse was Willow's fault.

"As if almost ending the world *once* wasn't bad enough," she whispered, fighting back the urge to cry.

"This is different," Dawn replied, appearing next to Willow, carrying a cardboard box filled with magick supplies. "Last time, you wanted to destroy the world. This time you didn't mean to. It's a totally different vibe."

Willow tried to smile for Dawn's sake. "It's still my fault," she said. "I knew if I used magick again I might hurt the people I love. I didn't think I'd be causing global devastation quite so soon, though. I'm an idiot."

She flipped the pages faster, barely even looking at what was written on them. Dawn took her hand and gently closed the book. "That one says 'Invisibility' on the cover," she pointed out. "I don't think it will explain why your levitation spell started the apocalypse."

Willow sighed. "I was thinking maybe my time as the invisible woman changed me somehow," she said. "You know, like it messed with my mojo and that's why my spell went wrong."

"I think the problem is you have too much mojo," Anya mumbled from the couch. "Let's go to your apartment and have sex," she suggested to Xander.

Dawn rolled her eyes. "We're in the middle of a crisis," she pointed out.

"Well, it's not like we can stop it now," Anya

replied. "These two made a mythological beast and it woke the angel of death. End of story. At least we can die satisfied," she added, reaching for Xander.

As usual, what Anya said was true. And as usual, Willow tried to ignore that fact. She couldn't shake the idea that she had to figure out *why* the levitation spell had gone wrong, that somehow she could fix things if only she knew exactly what had made them go haywire in the first place. But deep down, she knew she was looking for a larger explanation, or maybe vindication. She was hoping she'd find out it wasn't her fault, even though she felt with a sick certainty that it was.

Willow put aside the invisibility book and picked up another one. "'To Search for Lost Witches'," she read from the cover. "Why didn't you bring any, you know, general magick books?" she complained.

"I thought I was coming here to find you," Giles reminded her.

"Oh yeah," Willow said. "I guess you weren't expecting the end of the world."

"No one expects the Spanish Inquisition," Xander put in.

"Besides, Willow, you're the one who sucked all the info out of my book collection at the Magic Box," Anya said accusingly. "Book sucker."

Willow winced. It was true. When she'd been determined to destroy the world, she'd pretty much destroyed most of their reference materials in the process. "I know, I know," she said. "Sorry."

"You don't have many supplies," Dawn commented,

rummaging around in the cardboard box. "This is all I found in your room."

"Yeah. That's part of the whole easing-back-into-magick thing," Willow said. "I only got enough supplies for the one little levitation spell we were planning to do."

Dawn pulled out the small glass pot. "What's this?" she asked.

"Hog turds," Willow said. "For the spell."

"Hog turds?" Xander cried, leaping to his feet. "Excuse me? Hog turds?"

Busted! Willow shrugged, trying to look innocent. "The spell called for them."

"And did it say that I had to be the one to spread them all over the notebook?" he demanded. "I can't believe you, Will. Friends don't let friends touch pig poop."

"Hogs are different from pigs," Anya said.

"No, they're not," Giles cut in, trying to calm things down. "Pig, swine, and hog are synonyms."

"Missing the point!" Xander fumed. "I touched poo!"

"Sorry," Willow said again. She felt as if she'd spent the entire day apologizing. Would there ever come a time when she wouldn't feel she had to ask forgiveness for everything?

"Hey!" Anya snapped, suddenly abandoning Xander. She stomped across the living room and snatched the glass pot from Dawn's hand. "These hog turds aren't from the Magic Box!" She narrowed her eyes at Willow. "Where did you get them?"

"Um, mail order," Willow said. "From Phillippa's House of Enchantment."

Anya drew in a sharp breath, and her eyes filled with rage. Willow took a step back, expecting Anya's smooth skin to explode into vengeance-demon bumps at any moment. "You bought supplies from that charlatan?" she bellowed. "From my biggest competition?"

"Sorry," Willow said. It just didn't have the same impact when you'd already apologized twenty times in the past five minutes. "But, you know, it's not like she's your competition anymore."

"I don't care. That woman sells inferior goods!" Anya cried. "She sells in bulk and undercuts my earnings! She's an ogre who's driving independent magick shops out of business!"

"She's an ogre?" Dawn asked.

"She wishes!" Anya yelled. "I bet she doesn't even smell as good as an actual ogre! I can't stay here with this traitor," she added, turning away from Willow.

"But Anya, the Magic Box is closed," Willow said, trying to defend herself. "You're not in business anymore. I have to get supplies from somewhere."

"It's closed because the government wouldn't let me charge people money for goods in a place that could collapse on their heads," Anya said. "Because *you* trashed the whole building. *You* destroyed my livelihood!"

Xander winced. Even Willow had to admit that Anya had a point. She sighed. "Sorry," she mumbled.

• • •

"What are we doing again, exactly?" Spike asked. He pulled his black duster tighter around his body. It was an old habit—he couldn't really feel the frigid air. It was one of the advantages of being dead. But he knew it had turned cold again, really cold, since the sun went out. The few remaining humans in town had taken to lighting fires fueled by the wood of decaying trees. They huddled together and gazed suspiciously at Buffy and Spike as they passed. Spike couldn't care less about them. He kept his eyes on Buffy. Her breath fogged in the air, and tiny snowflakes coated her golden hair.

"We're finding Michael," she said, her teeth chattering.

"Riiight," Spike replied. He couldn't even think of that hideous monster without wanting to retch. "Why?"

Buffy went on walking, fast. Spike kept pace with her easily, even though he couldn't think of a single reason to hurry. The world was ending. Why not take things easy, enjoy a stroll? Enjoy each other's company.

"To tell him about Willow and Xander. Of course he couldn't be sitting in the diner like usual," Buffy said. She hugged herself, rubbing her arms to fight off the chill. "I can't believe how cold it is," she added. "Is this how people feel in Alaska all the time?"

Spike pulled off his duster and placed it gently around her shoulders. "I wouldn't know," he said. "Not enough people in Alaska for good hunting."

Buffy shot him an annoyed look.

"What?" he said. "I'm a vampire. I went where the food was. Besides, Alaska always sounded bloody boring to me."

"There!" Buffy cried. She pointed to a stucco building on the corner of Main Street. Spike squinted at it. It had obviously been a bank, and it had obviously been looted.

"Damn shame," he agreed. "I don't know what people think money's going to do against all this carnage and mayhem."

"That's not what I mean," Buffy said. "Look at the shadows!"

Sure enough, there was a faint glow on the wall of the bank, against which Spike could make out a few shadows so subtle that it was impossible to tell what was casting them. "And?" he asked.

"It's a zombie," Buffy said excitedly. "One of the glowy ones!"

"Oh, goody," Spike replied dryly. Those zombies freaked him out. The nonglowing kind were fine. They tried to grab people and eat their brains, just as zombies should. But the glowing ones didn't act like proper zombies at all. They just walked around in a daze, following that Michael creature.

Suddenly Spike understood. "It'll lead us right to Mr. Apocalypse. The bloke's like catnip to them."

Buffy nodded. "I think the glowing ones are people he's judged to be good. So they follow him."

"And the nonglowing zombies are just the baddies. They can't stand the sight of him," Spike said. "I guess I should go hang out with them, then."

Buffy stopped walking and turned to face him. It was so unexpected that he almost barreled straight into her.

"Look, Spike," she said seriously. "Michael thinks it's his job to be the judge."

"Well, he's a pretty literal one," Spike said. "No wiggle room in his definitions."

"So he thinks you're wicked," Buffy said. "So what? When have you ever cared what people think of you?"

Spike wasn't sure what to say. The truth was that he'd always cared what people thought. He'd cared too much. Old wounds to his pride still stung—being mocked by the elegant ladies he'd grown up with, being bested by Angel in a fight. Being rejected by Buffy when all he wanted was to love her. "All I know is, your new boyfriend should look a little deeper at people before he decides if they're good or bad," he muttered.

"I agree." Buffy turned and headed toward the bank.

Spike stared after her, taken aback. He'd expected her to leap to Michael's defense. "She's always surprising," he said admiringly. Then he ran to catch up. "So what's the plan?" he asked.

"This is all a big mistake," Buffy said. "And when I explain that to Michael, he'll stop the apocalypse."

"Just like that, huh?" Spike couldn't help feeling that she was being naïve.

"Yeah, just like that." Buffy stuck her chin in the air and began taking longer strides. She'd gone into powerful, you-can't-stop-me mode. Spike recognized it instantly. There was no point in arguing with her when she was in a mood like this.

"Well, I hope you're right," he said. "Because it would be just my luck to get my soul back right in time to see it go straight to a hell dimension for all eternity."

Buffy didn't answer. She was intent on the glowing zombie up ahead. The corpse had once been a Latina woman, and she still had the scars from the car accident that had killed her. But her face was peaceful, and the soft yellow glow surrounding her seemed to shield her from any awareness that she was now the walking dead. *Some people will swallow anything,* Spike thought in disgust. Wandering around in your own personal spotlight wouldn't be his idea of resting in peace.

The zombie was shuffling slowly down Main Street, ignoring the burnt-out cars and the shattered glass of the looted shops. As she passed the bank, the light on the stucco wall diminished and darkness returned to the side street they were on. Buffy was heading for Main Street—she was clearly going to follow the zombie straight to Michael. But Spike liked the darkness here. He had a sudden unreasonable fear that the instant they turned onto Main Street, he'd be surrounded by those glowing corpses. Or worse, that he'd have to face Michael. A shiver of fear ran through him at the thought.

It's much safer to stay right here, a voice whispered in his head. *You can be with Buffy again after she's had her little chat with Michael.*

Spike tried to shake it off. One thing he had never been was a coward, and he wasn't about to start now. Buffy wasn't afraid of Michael, so why should he be? She had just turned the corner onto Main Street, disappearing from his sight. He steeled himself and followed her.

As soon as he stepped onto the major roadway, Spike's breath began to come in gasps. Four more glowing zombies meandered through the remnants of what had been downtown Sunnydale, picking their way around the rent asphalt and climbing over fallen streetlamps and trees. But none of that bothered Spike. What bothered him was the man standing at the end of the street, on the steps of City Hall. Michael.

He stood still, watching them approach. Just standing there, not doing anything threatening. He had no weapon. He gave no indication of wanting to attack. And yet Spike began to feel lightheaded. *Run!* the voice in his head screamed over and over again. His cold skin felt even clammier than usual.

"I'm going to stay with Buffy," he said aloud. "This bloke can't do anything to me."

Through sheer force of will, he wrenched his eyes up to Michael's face. Hideous. It was grotesque. Bright blue eyes that seemed to almost burn through him. A wave of revulsion shot through Spike, making him feel sick to his stomach. Fear washed over him. *Get out of here!* the voice cried, more insistently.

"There's nothing to be afraid of," he said through clenched teeth. But he couldn't help it; he felt like a baby mouse cornered by the baddest tomcat in history. Just being within a hundred yards of Michael filled him with the sort of panic he hadn't known since he was human. It wasn't normal for a vampire to be so afraid. It wasn't right.

Buffy was staring at him. She stood twenty feet away, watching him with an air of impatience. "Are you coming?" she asked.

Spike swallowed. "Sure," he croaked. He took a step forward, then another. He kept his eyes on Buffy and tried not to think about the fact that he was walking closer to the most fearsome monster he'd ever laid eyes on.

Buffy turned and kept walking, just bouncing along toward Michael as if everything were fine. How could she do it? Why didn't she see this so-called angel for what he was? She thought he was beautiful. The guy was starting the bloody apocalypse, but still she thought he was beautiful!

I trust Buffy, Spike thought. If Buffy considered this Michael person to be good company, then that was enough for Spike. Just thinking about Buffy lessened the overwhelming fear a tiny bit. He wanted to stay near her, wanted to be there for her when she needed a comrade-in-arms. Spike put on a burst of speed, jogging up to Buffy. He reached out for her arm, but as he did, he caught a glimpse of Michael over her shoulder. He was smiling, a terrifying grin filled with gleaming white fangs, the very light of which burned like the sun.

Run! his inner voice screamed, and he did.

• • •

Spike's strangled cry caught Buffy by surprise. By the time she spun around, he was already disappearing back around the corner. Buffy heaved a sigh. Should she follow him? He was obviously terrified of Michael. Maybe she could comfort him.

But she wasn't sure that was her place anymore. And truthfully, she'd never done girlfriend-y things like that even when they were . . . together. Besides, she had to talk to Michael as soon as she could. She'd just have to make sure later that Spike was okay.

Buffy turned back to look at Michael standing on the steps of City Hall. He took her breath away. Each time she saw him he seemed to become more gorgeous. It was as if the contrast with the devastated world around him brought his beauty into sharper focus. Buffy felt butterflies in her stomach as she practically skipped toward him. He was already watching her with a gentle smile. It would be so wonderful to be able to have a pleasant conversation with him for a change, to bring him good news.

"Hi, Buffy!" he called as she approached.

"Hi," she answered. She could feel the idiotic grin on her face and she felt powerless to stop it, even though it was a free-will grin. "I have good news," she burst out.

Michael raised his eyebrows. "*Good* news?" he asked skeptically, gazing out over the destruction.

"Huh," Buffy said, tilting her head to the side. "I didn't know angels could be snarky."

His sky blue eyes clouded with confusion, and Buffy laughed. "Yes, good news," she said. "You can stop now."

"What do you mean?" he asked.

"The apocalypse," she explained. "It's a false alarm."

Michael sighed. "Buffy—"

"I know what you're gonna say," she interrupted. "You're gonna tell me it's wishful thinking."

"I was going to say denial," he said.

"But it's not," Buffy said in a rush. The relief inside her was so great that she felt giddy. "Your sign—the wolf in sheep's clothing? I saw it. Again, I mean. I saw it today."

"I thought you killed it when you first saw it," Michael said.

"I did," she assured him. "But they made another one. Willow and Xander." She stopped talking and waited for his reaction. He just gazed at her blankly. "Willow and Xander," she repeated. "They're the ones who made the sign. The wolf-sheep. The shoolf. The weep." Buffy couldn't help noticing that Michael didn't seem amused. Or relieved. Or even the least bit curious. In fact, he looked kind of sad.

"Buffy . . . ," he started.

"Okay, I'll be serious," she said. "I'm just so happy. They were doing a levitation spell or something, and it went wrong, and they made the wolf. And the sheep. All at once."

"So?" Michael asked.

"*So,* it was an accident," she said. He might be

beautiful, but he certainly was dense. "It doesn't count."

Michael sighed. "Yes, it does," he said.

Buffy was getting frustrated. Why was it so hard for him to understand? "It wasn't a true sign," she said slowly, as if talking to a four-year-old. "It was just a stupid spell gone wrong."

"A spell that created a wolf in sheep's clothing," Michael said.

"Exactly!" Buffy cried. "So, see, it wasn't a *real* wolf in sheep's clothing."

"Of course it was," he replied. "You saw it. You fought it."

"Well, yeah. Okay, so it was real," she said. "But it wasn't the sign."

"Why not?" Michael asked.

Buffy wanted to answer. It seemed as if the answer was so obvious, so crystal clear. But somehow she couldn't find the words. The wolf that her friends had made couldn't be a sign of the apocalypse because . . . well, just because.

"It doesn't matter where the sign came from," Michael told her. "Only that it came."

"Of course it matters!" Buffy snapped. "Two people doing a dumb magick spell do not create giant world-ending omens."

"Willow's magick has had some pretty serious consequences before," Michael pointed out.

"That was different!" Buffy cried. "She meant to do it then. This time·was an accident."

"But why should that matter, Buffy?" he asked

mildly. "Why can't the final sign come about accidentally?"

"Because the world shouldn't end accidentally," Buffy said through clenched teeth. Michael was treating this conversation just like any of their other discussions, as if it were nothing more than an intellectual argument. His calmness made her want to scream.

"Aren't accidents a part of life?" he asked. "Aren't they a part of the world? Why can't it end that way?"

"Look," Buffy said. "I don't know who you work for. I don't know who sent you here and told you to look for your little lamb-wolf thing. But whoever it is, whatever it is, I can't believe it wants the world to end over something this . . . this stupid."

"Try to understand," he said. "Willow and Xander were part of the plan. Their spell going wrong was part of it, too."

"I don't understand that," she retorted. "It's not all planned. My life hasn't been one big plan."

"How do you know?"

Buffy answered without thinking. "Because it's been messy and scary and filled with death. Because why would some higher power have me saving the world all the time when it was going to end so soon anyway?"

Michael stared at her for a moment, speechless. Buffy couldn't believe it. She'd stumped him!

"You know it's true," she pressed. "Maybe someday there was supposed to be a sign to wake you up. But not now, not like this. This is just a big mistake."

He shook his head. "It doesn't work that way.

Maybe there wasn't a plan, but the sign was still the right sign."

"That's insane!" Buffy exploded. "The wolf thing was an accident. This apocalypse is an . . . an over-reaction. You jumped the gun."

"My job is very specific," he argued. "I see the sign, I start the end time."

"But that wasn't the sign," she insisted. "It came from the wrong place."

"Interpreting who sent the sign isn't my job," he said.

If I could hit him, I think I would right about now, Buffy thought. How could Michael be so stubborn when the world was at stake? "Fine," she said aloud. "Whose job is it?"

Michael's fair skin turned ever-so-slightly paler. "I don't know," he admitted.

"Well, who's your boss?" she asked.

He looked at her sadly. "There is no boss. There is no appeals court. I know only my piece of the puzzle."

"I don't understand," Buffy said.

"This is how it is," he replied helplessly. "How it has always been. This is the way the world is set up."

"By whom?" Buffy asked.

"It's how it is," he repeated. "I don't know the an-swers to the eternal questions any more than you do."

"And no one ever gave you a number to call if things went wrong?"

Michael shook his head. "Things haven't gone wrong, Buffy. There has never been a wolf in sheep's clothing before. Your friends created one. However it happened, however the world reached that point . . . they created the sign to awaken me."

Her throat tightened as if he were strangling her. "So you're not going to stop it?" Buffy whispered.

"I'm sorry," Michael replied, "but no."

CHAPTER ELEVEN

"**D**id you find anything when you did your search?" Giles asked, peering over Willow's shoulder. He tried to keep his attention focused on Willow and her research. He didn't want to think about Buffy and what he suspected she was finding out from Michael.

"Nope," Willow answered. "I've searched for levitation spells in every branch of magick, and none of them mention wolf creation as a side effect."

"Maybe it wasn't the spell. Maybe it was *you*," Anya muttered in Willow's direction. Giles sighed. She'd been sulking on the couch ever since discovering that Willow had used Phillippa's House of Enchantment. He had to admit, that rankled. He didn't find himself agreeing with Anya on many occasions, but

Phillippa had stolen more business from him than he cared to remember. It wasn't as if Willow had a choice, of course, but he could understand Anya's frustration.

Xander let out a belch, then held up a glass of maggot-strained Coke as an explanation.

"Could Anya be right?" Willow asked. "Do you think that's possible, Giles? Could I have somehow made the wolf through subconscious dark magick?"

"It doesn't matter," Buffy said from the doorway.

Giles turned to see her looking drained. Her eyes were even more haunted than usual.

"Why doesn't it matter?" Xander asked.

"Buffy, what happened?" Giles asked gently, although he knew the answer. He could see it on her face.

"I talked to Michael," she answered. "I told him to stop the apocalypse. I mean, the wolf thing was just a freak accident, right?"

"I can't find any reason for it," Willow said. "So that seems kinda freak accident-y to me."

"Well, that's what I told him," Buffy went on. "But he didn't care."

"He said the wolf in sheep's clothing was still the sign," Giles guessed. "No matter where it came from."

Buffy raised her teary eyes to his. "He wouldn't listen to reason," she said. "Any chance you guys found out he's a big, bad demon in disguise and now you know how I can kill him?"

Her sad expression was almost more than he could take. "I'm sorry. I stayed up all last night searching for anything. . . . But while different cultures and religions call him by different names, Michael is the being cho-sen long ago to bring about the end of days." His voice had begun to shake a little, and he cleared his throat. "It is simply time."

"Time for what?" Buffy cried, a tear spilling onto her cheek. Giles couldn't tell if she was crying from anger or from fear. Probably both. "Time to kill us all?"

"I don't see why it ever has to be time for *that*," Anya chimed in.

"This is beyond our control," Giles said. He looked at their faces—Willow, so worried that she'd done something wrong; Dawn, looking to him for answers; Xander and Anya, trying to cling on to some shred of hope. And Buffy. He could see it in her eyes, in the way she held her muscles taut—she wanted to fight. It was killing her that she couldn't beat this enemy. He hated being the one to have to tell them this. It went against everything inside of him to give up hope. Even when faced with the darkest dangers, he'd never been hopeless before. But this time was different. This enemy was different.

He took off his glasses and sank down onto the arm of the couch. "Try to understand," he said gently. "I know you've all been struggling to accept this, but it's time to stop struggling. We shouldn't be fighting this apocalypse."

"We fight all the other ones," Dawn replied.

"I know." Giles sought out Buffy's eyes. He held her gaze. "But this is the real one. The natural one. The *good* one."

"How can the end of the world be good?" Buffy whispered.

"Because it has to end sometime," he said. "Every single religion that has ever existed on earth has had a myth of the end time. That alone should tell us that there is supposed to be an end."

"I keep thinking about what Xander said before," Dawn jumped in. "Why didn't we just let it all end one of the other times? Buffy died to stop the world from being destroyed. She killed Angel! All that's happened is that she's gotten hurt again and again for nothing!"

"Because those were wrong, unnatural endings," Giles replied, struggling to find a way to make a child understand something that was difficult for he himself to fully accept. "Endings that could, theoretically, have plunged us all into a hell dimension forevermore."

"Then what's going to happen this time?" Willow asked.

"I don't know," he admitted. "While religions generally agree on what happens before the end, they diverge radically on what happens *after* the end."

"Well, that's not very helpful," Xander said.

"No it's not," Giles agreed. "I think we'll just have to rely on our own personal beliefs about what happens next." He glanced at Buffy. She hadn't said much. "It's not giving up, Buffy," he told her. "If this is meant to happen, then it's beyond your control. You can't fight it. As hard as it is, we have to try to accept that."

"That's what Michael keeps telling me," she said.

Dawn went over and slipped her arm around her sister. "Maybe he's right. This way you can stop getting hurt," she said. "You can't fight everything, Buffy. You're not God."

What more was there to try? Michael's force field couldn't be broken. There were zombies crawling all over the entire earth. And more than that, even without his mojo working on her, Michael felt *good*. Maybe her work was really finally done. Maybe there was a true and natural end to this world and they had reached it.

Buffy nodded, and her body relaxed. "Okay," she mumbled. "I can't fight it."

It broke Giles's heart to see her give up, even though he felt sure it was the right thing to do. "We have to try to remember that this is all right," Giles said. "The end time was decided before the world was even born. And whatever does happen, at least we'll all be together."

"For now, maybe," Anya said bitterly. "With all this judging going on, I doubt we'll be together afterward."

Giles felt a pang of sympathy for Anya. She might be a vengeance demon, and she might be completely impossible as a human, but she'd had a difficult year. He put his arm around her shoulders. "Maybe it's only for now," he told her, "but we are together." He held his other arm out to Buffy, and she moved into his embrace. Slowly, one by one, the others joined the hug.

It was strange to think how important these young people had become to him over the years. Giles couldn't imagine being without them now. He closed his eyes and held them as tightly as he could. They were his family.

• • •

Buffy held on to the others with all her strength. These were the people she loved most in the world, and all that mattered was that she was with them, safe in their arms. *Soon it will be over,* she thought. Maybe she would go back to heaven after the end. Or wherever it was that she'd gone last time. How strange it was that she'd actually been dead and had an afterlife, and yet she still didn't know for sure what happened when you died. Holding tight to her little sister and her best friends, Buffy tried to concentrate on remembering. What had it been like, that place? It hadn't really been a place at all. It was more like a mind-set, a way of being. It was the best memory she had, but try as she might, she couldn't make it come clear.

Her mom had been there, she was pretty sure of that. Not that they'd had long mother-daughter chats or anything. But Buffy definitely remembered finally feeling at peace about her mom's death. She'd known that Joyce was okay, and she'd known that she was okay too. That everyone she loved would be taken care of, that she had nothing to worry about, not ever. She had done her job. Maybe she'd go back to that place when this was over. Maybe the others would go there with her. That wouldn't be so bad.

But it wasn't right. Even the idea of being back there, at peace, didn't comfort her. Usually when she thought about that heavenly place, she felt an intense longing for it. But right now all she felt was sad. *It isn't fair,* she thought. It had taken her so long to get over having been dead. After Willow brought her back to life, all she'd wanted was to reverse it. To get back to heaven. For almost a year she'd felt that way, until Dawn had finally helped her see that being alive had its good points too, until Buffy had finally realized that she wanted to live. And that had only been a few months ago. It wasn't enough time.

But what was she supposed to do about it? Giles was right; she couldn't fight this apocalypse. Michael had tried to tell her the same thing many times. It was time for her to let go. To let someone else take responsibility. Her job was done.

The thought sent a shudder through her. Ever since she was called to be the Slayer, she'd resented it a little. She'd had to take on burdens far too big for one girl. She hadn't had the luxury of a normal life. Instead she'd been fighting against unimaginable odds for years. She'd always thought it would be a relief to let go of being the Slayer, to just be normal again, but now that that time had come, she wasn't sure she could actually do it. How could her job be done? What was she without her job, anyway?

Nothing. Nobody. It wasn't a job. It was who she was, what she was, why she existed. Buffy drew in a breath, feeling the air rush into her lungs, filling her with life. She was the Slayer. At this moment she felt connected to every other Slayer who ever had been and who ever would be. The Slayer was born to protect, born to fight. Without the fight she was nothing.

Panic rose up inside of her. How could she face what was coming? Was she supposed to sit around and wait? But what would she do while waiting? How would she keep the panic at bay? Fear coursed through her veins. She'd never done this before. When she first found out about the demons and monsters who walked the earth, she also found out about her innate ability to fight them. She'd been frightened at first, but there was always the fight to distract her, to keep her focused. What was she supposed to do without a fight? Just . . . just be afraid?

"No!" Buffy gasped. She jerked away from the others, breathing hard.

"Jeez, Buff, we're just trying to help," Xander said.

"No," she said, still panicked. "I can't do this. I don't sit around and wait for the world to end. I can't. I have to fight it."

They all stared back at her uncertainly. But now her uncertainty was gone. She looked Giles in the eye. "It's what I do," she told him. "Even if this apocalypse is supposed to happen, I have to fight it. I have to, Giles."

He was silent for a moment, studying her with an unreadable expression. Then he smiled, and Buffy knew he was with her. He understood.

"Thank god somebody said that," Anya muttered.

Willow grinned. "Leave it to the Buffster to go for violence over acceptance."

Xander ruffled Buffy's hair. "That's our girl," he agreed.

"Yeah. Yay," Dawn put in. "But, um, what do we do now?"

Buffy gave her sister an affectionate shove. "We go stop the world from ending, silly."

"I know. I'm down with that," Dawn said. "I just mean . . . how do we do it? This apocalypse is still the good apocalypse, right?"

"Well, I don't know that the apocalypse itself can be described as good," Giles replied. "But the forces bringing it about are good. This isn't an untimely, unnatural destruction—"

"Right, so it's good," Dawn interrupted. "And that's what I'm talking about. Buffy, you've fought all kinds of evil. But how are we supposed to fight the forces of good?"

"Okay, so the ancient Sumerians also didn't think there was a way to stop the end time," Willow reported, closing the Web page she'd been studying. She was trying to keep her voice upbeat, but one look at her friends' faces made that impossible. They were all sprawled around the living room, staring morosely at her. They'd been trying to come up with a plan for three hours with no luck. "But, hey, we're only on the *S*'s," she said cheerfully. "Who knows, maybe the Zoroastrians will have an idea for us."

"Oh, be quiet," Anya said. "It's hopeless."

"Come on, Anya," Xander told her. "There's always hope."

"I think our best hope was sweet-talking Michael," Buffy said. "And I totally failed at that."

"Maybe someone else should try," Anya suggested. "Buffy isn't good at flirting."

"I don't think angels respond to flirting," Willow said. "I mean, they're kind of above it, aren't they?"

"I wish we could just go blow him up with something," Dawn burst out. "That would make him stop."

Willow knew Dawn was scared, but the suggestion still shocked her. "But, Dawnie, it would also make us angel killers," she pointed out.

"How are we supposed to fight him if we can't *fight* him?" Dawn complained.

"It wouldn't do any good to try to attack Michael," Buffy said grimly. "He's protected, remember? Nothing can harm him." Her voice was strained. "But we have to think of something. We're running out of time."

Willow swallowed hard. Her friends had all fallen back into depression. No one was even offering new ideas anymore. There weren't any good ideas. *Should I mention the siphon?* Willow wondered. No, that wasn't a good idea either. She turned back to the computer.

But all she could do was stare at the screen. Her mind was filled with fear. Just the very thought of the siphon spell had sent her brain into a tailspin. She noticed Giles giving her a strange look and tried to shake off her fear. "What comes after *S*?" she murmured. "*T*. Let's check the Talmud." She typed in a search request. As various pages full of Talmudic lore filled the screen Willow lapsed back into mute terror. The siphon spell might be their only chance to stop Armageddon. But how could she suggest doing such a thing? A spell like that might just end the world on its own. It was better not to mention it. Besides, she couldn't do that spell. She wasn't strong enough—the spell might turn her back into out-of-control, friend-hurting Willow. She couldn't risk it. It was just too frightening.

"Amazing, really," Giles said, reading over her shoulder. "How long will it work?"

"It won't work," Willow snapped. "It's too dangerous."

He raised his eyebrows, and Willow realized that he wasn't talking about the siphon spell. "Um . . . what?" she asked lamely.

"The Internet," Giles said, still looking at her in surprise. "How long will it work?"

"Oh." Willow felt like an idiot. She pushed away thoughts of the siphon. "Um . . . until the end, probably. It was started by the military as a way to keep communication going no matter what happened. It's supposed to be nuclear war resistant."

"Hmm," Giles sniffed. "Like a cockroach."

The front door opened, and Spike appeared with a plastic grocery bag. "I found water," he announced. "No maggots. Don't know why." He pulled a gallon jug of water from the bag and handed it to Buffy.

"Where'd you find it?" she asked, ripping off the plastic cap.

"Little market outside town," Spike replied. "No maggots in the whole place."

"Maybe the apocalypse is breaking down on its own," Xander said. "Because it started with a sign from the wrong place."

"Michael said that didn't matter," Buffy reminded him, handing the water jug to Dawn.

"Well, how else do you explain it?" Xander argued.

"I can't explain it, all right?" Buffy snapped. "I'm not an apocalypse expert."

"Well, someone better be," Anya put in. "It was your idea to try to fight it. Why don't you have a plan?"

"Leave her alone!" Dawn cried.

"Yeah," Xander agreed. "Buffy's the fighter, she's not the brains."

"Hey!" Spike snarled. "She's got more brains than you, mate."

"Stop it!" Willow yelled. All eyes turned to her. She felt her cheeks redden. "Fighting with one another is pointless," she said. They all kept looking at her. She knew that tensions were running high because they were all scared. The decision to fight the apocalypse had brought a new energy to the group, but it wasn't enough. They needed a plan. And it seemed as if she was the only one who had one.

"I have an idea," she said. "It's a spell—" Her voice failed. The very thought of working this magick made her numb with fear.

"What spell?" Anya asked impatiently. Willow just stared at her. No words could penetrate the fear.

"Will?" Xander said gently. He came over and took her hand. She clung onto him, focusing her attention on the warmth of his hand, the certainty of his friendship calming her. She looked up at him. "I'm afraid," she said.

"Just tell us about the spell," he replied. "You don't have to do anything magickal right now."

Willow nodded. "It's an undo spell," she said. "I thought we could maybe undo the levitation spell that created the wolf in sheep's clothing."

Buffy stepped forward and took Willow's other

hand. "That sounds like a good idea," she said.

"But it means using magick, powerful magick," Willow said.

"You're up to it, Will. You're strong enough," Buffy told her.

"You don't understand," Willow cried. "This is serious magick, the strongest kind there is. If I try it, I'm afraid . . . I'm afraid I'll lose myself again." She could feel Giles's eyes on her.

"What spell is this?" he asked in a voice that told her he already knew the answer.

"The Belial siphon," she whispered.

Silence fell over the room. When she looked up, she could see that the color had drained from Giles's face. Anya and Spike were both staring at her openmouthed.

"I told you it was powerful magick," she said.

Spike snorted. "Magick my ass," he said. "It's a myth."

"No it's not," Anya put in. "It's just impossible for anyone to do."

"Um, hello?" Dawn said. "What are you guys talking about?"

"The Belial siphon is the stuff of legend," Giles explained. "The most powerful of all spells, never to be used lightly. Never to be used at all, in fact." Willow couldn't tell from his voice whether or not he thought she was crazy for even mentioning it.

"Why would there be a spell that can't be used?" Xander sputtered. "What's the point of that?"

"Why can't we use it?" Buffy asked. "What does it do?"

"It undoes everything, that's what I heard," Anya said. "It undoes the fabric of reality."

"That's what the Watchers Council says too, in a manner of speaking," Giles agreed. "The Belial siphon reverses magick, but it also reverses actions, thoughts . . . time itself."

"So it's like Superman flying backward around the earth and reversing its rotation to turn back time," Xander put in.

"Exactly," Spike said.

Buffy, Dawn, Anya, and Giles looked blankly at them. Spike's eyes widened. Embarrassed, he turned to Xander. "What are you talking about?" he demanded.

"*Superman: The Movie*," Willow said. She didn't share her best friend's taste in comic books, but she'd certainly spent enough time watching cheesy old movies with him when they were kids. She smiled at Xander. "I think that's exactly what it does. It's an undo spell, but you can't make it undo one specific thing. If you work the Belial siphon, it undoes everything."

"Everything since when?" Dawn asked. "I mean, would it undo everything that happened since you worked the levitation spell? Or would it go back further and undo everything for the past month?"

Willow felt the fear pushing its way back up inside of her. "I don't know," she said in a trembling voice.

"That's why it's such dangerous magick," Giles commented. "It can't be controlled. You work the spell to set it off, but then it does whatever it wants. You can't dictate the terms. The siphon will undo however much it decides to undo."

"But that could mean everything," Buffy said. "It could undo everything that's ever happened throughout history?"

"Theoretically," Giles answered. "No one really knows."

"No self-respecting demon would even think of using that kind of magick," Anya said. "It destroys everything, good and bad."

"So it's like the nuclear bomb of magick spells," Xander said. "No one wants to use it because it could destroy its user along with its target."

"Exactly," Giles said. "If we were to work the Belial siphon in order to undo Willow's botched levitation spell, there's no telling what kind of side effects the siphon itself would cause."

"What happened last time someone used it?" Dawn asked.

Willow frowned. "I don't know," she said. She glanced at Spike.

"Don't ask me," he said. "I thought the bloody thing was nothing but a myth."

"As far as I know, no one has ever worked the Belial siphon," Giles said, wrinkling his brow in concentration. "I can't remember reading anything about it actually being used."

"Me neither," Willow said.

"Then how do we know it's so bad?" Buffy demanded.

Willow shrugged. Ever since she'd first started studying magick, she'd heard bits and pieces of information about the Belial siphon. It was like the boogeyman of spells—something other Wiccans whispered about and feared. But no one had ever given her any hard facts about it. "Everyone says it's really bad," she answered lamely.

"The Council placed a strict ban against the use of the Belial siphon," Giles said. "The potential for devastating side effects was too great to risk."

"Side effects like what?" Buffy asked.

"Well, what we've been saying," Willow replied. "You know, undoing all civilization, undoing evolution or the movement of the tectonic plate. Who knows? It could totally destroy the world."

"You mean, like Michael is about to do?" Buffy asked.

Willow thought about that. "Well, I don't think it could really *end* the world, but it could *undo* the world."

"That doesn't sound much worse than what we've got," Buffy said.

"It's still risky," Giles told her. "We could inadvertently make things worse. Send us all to a—"

"A hell dimension, I know," Buffy said. "But if this siphon spell thingy just undoes everything, it shouldn't be able to send us where we've never been before. Right?"

Willow tried to figure out if that made sense. And the answer was, she didn't know. Nothing really seemed to make sense anymore. She shot a glance at Giles. He shrugged.

"I—I think that's right," she said.

"Great!" Buffy chirped. "Let's do it."

"We've got nothing to lose," Xander said. "What do we need, Will?"

Willow could barely hear him over the rushing sound in her ears. They were going to do the Belial siphon? The most dangerous, powerful spell of all time? *She* was going to do it? "I don't know," she gasped. "I don't know what we need." She couldn't seem to get her mind to work. It was too busy picturing all the ways such a powerful spell could push her off the magickal wagon again.

"Well, where's the ingredient list?" Xander asked.

Willow shrugged helplessly. "There isn't one."

"Why not?" Dawn asked.

"I'm not entirely sure the Belial siphon has ever been written down," Giles said mildly.

Spike barked out a laugh. "I told you it was just a story," he said. "The spell doesn't even exist."

"It must exist somewhere," Willow said, trying to force her mind to focus. "It may have been passed down orally. Some spells are never written because just to commit them to paper would be too dangerous."

"It must be more complicated than just some spell you read," Buffy said. "How are we supposed to find out how to do it if there's no record of it?"

Willow knew the answer to that one. But it meant using more magick. So she kept her mouth shut.

"A discovery spell, perhaps?" Giles said to her.

She nodded. Giles patted her arm, understanding her fear. He'd been with her all through her rehab in England. She wondered if he was as unsure of her magickal stability as she was.

"One thing we'll certainly need for the Belial siphon is a fire pot," Giles said. "The oldest spells always need fire. Anya, there used to be one or two at the Magic Box. I don't suppose they're still there?"

"I had some on order when Willow ruined the shop," Anya said pointedly. "But I think there may have been one left in the storeroom."

"Let's go get it, then," Xander told her.

"Excellent," Giles said. "Then Willow and I will get started on the discovery spell."

"I'll go find Michael," Buffy put in. "Maybe I can stall him."

"And how do you plan to do that?" Spike asked.

"I'm not sure," Buffy admitted. "He likes to have philosophical discussions. Maybe I can get him started on the ethics of killing spiders. That should take awhile."

"Okay, we have a plan," Dawn said happily. Willow could see that the others were re-energized. But all she felt was dread.

CHAPTER TWELVE

"**G**lowing corpse, three o'clock," Spike told Buffy. They were wandering through the campus of UC Sunnydale, which looked like a battleground. The first dorm they'd passed was boarded up from the inside, as if the students were trying to keep the rapidly dissolving world from invading. Meanwhile, fraternity boys were roaming the campus, clearly drunk and looking for a fight.

"Have you noticed that there are fewer glowy guys wandering around?" Buffy said. "This is the first one we've seen since we left the house."

Spike nodded. "And the crowds around your boy keep getting bigger and bigger," he said. "They stick close to him once they find him."

"He's not my boy," Buffy told him.

"Whatever," Spike replied. But it made him happy just to hear her say that. He hadn't known if he'd ever be able to work with her like this—comfortable-like. Not after everything they'd been through. Sometimes it seemed as if she'd only been with him so she could hate herself. And maybe she still hated herself a little when she looked at him now.

But that wasn't all that was there. Since he'd gotten his soul back, there was something else between him and Buffy. Not pity. He bloody well wouldn't be able to stand that. He'd leave town if that was all she felt for him. It wasn't that. There was something else there. She cared for him in some deep way. He could feel it. And if all he could have was fighting on her side, he'd take it.

"It's heading toward the dining hall," Buffy said, stepping off the cement pathway to follow the glowing dead man across the dead grass. Spike trailed her.

"You don't have to come with me," Buffy told him. "It could be dangerous."

"What, you think I'm scared of that pansy? Please," Spike said.

Buffy rolled her eyes. "And you ran from him because . . . ?"

"All right, just because he's so ugly," Spike muttered. As if it wasn't bad enough that Michael had judged him to be wicked, now the guy was embarrassing him in front of Buffy.

"Spike, it's okay," she said. "To you he's a monster. He's dangerous and nasty and scary. If you weren't afraid of him, you wouldn't be normal."

He shrugged. "I still don't fancy looking like a coward to you," he said simply.

She slipped her arm through his, throwing him off guard. "You'll never be a coward to me," she said. "You've fought at my side a hundred times."

Spike was so surprised at the unexpected physical contact that he didn't know how to answer. Buffy had never been one for showing him affection even when they were involved. What did it mean that she was touching him now? He tried to analyze the touch: just light pressure, their arms linked. Could be nothing more than a friendly gesture. Could be more of a boyfriend and girlfriend thing. Was she hitting on him? He gave her a sideways glance, but she wasn't looking at him. *Should I try to hold her hand?* he wondered. She might hit him. But then again, that sometimes led to good times with Buffy. . . .

"Spike?" she said. "Why are you staring at me?"

"Oh, sorry." He immediately tore his eyes away and kept walking as if everything were perfectly normal. "Just thinking about how to stall the so-called angel."

Buffy stopped. "There's the rest of them," she said quietly.

Spike followed her gaze to the windows of the dining hall. The glass doors were open, and the entire place appeared to be filled with glowing zombies. They all stood around, staring in one direction—at Michael. Spike could just make out the small figure at the center of the glowing crowd, but that was enough.

He felt his skin crawl even looking at Michael from this far away.

Buffy tightened her grasp on his arm. "I have to go talk to him," she said. "You don't have to come with me."

"But I want to," he burst out. "I want to be with you as much as I can now."

Buffy searched his face. "What do you mean?"

"Just in case," Spike said. "In case the Belial siphon doesn't work. Because if that cracker ends the world, I get the feeling that you and I won't be seeing each other afterward."

"What are you talking about?" Buffy asked. "Why not? I mean, maybe afterward we'll all be together in some other dimension . . . or . . . or something."

"This guy is into judging," Spike pointed out. "Everything is all about who's good and who's wicked. Way I see it, that's gotta mean something. Like the old heaven and hell idea."

"We don't know that," Buffy said. "You heard Giles—Michael isn't a figure from any particular religion—"

"I know, love," Spike said gently. "But he's separating good from bad. He's been doing it all along." He nodded toward a nonglowing zombie stumbling across the wasted lawn, alone and adrift, unlike the hordes of others inside glowing together so that their light would surround Michael like a halo. "You're good. I'm wicked. It stands to reason that we'll be separated too."

Buffy stared at him, lips slightly parted in surprise. "I never thought of that," she said. "Not about what it meant after."

"Yeah, well, it don't matter to you, does it," he said bitterly. "But you're pretty much all I have to live for, so I'd like to maximize the time we have."

Buffy reached out to touch his cheek. "Spike, I'm sorry," she said. "I don't know what's going to happen, but I want you to know I don't think it's fair. I've done some things that I think qualify me as bad. And you have a soul now, which qualifies you as good in my book." She hesitated. "Maybe not good, but at least neutral."

He smiled. "I think that's the nicest thing you've ever said to me."

Buffy smiled back, but her eyes were sad. "Thank you for getting a soul for me," she said. "I know it's kinda torturing you, but it was an incredible thing to do."

Spike had to look away. He wasn't used to her being so sweet to him. "Lot of good it did me," he muttered. "Get my soul, the world ends."

She laughed. "Maybe your getting a soul was the real start of the apocalypse," she joked.

"I've been blamed for worse."

Buffy turned back to the glowing dining hall. "I have to go," she said. "You get as close to him as you can without freaking out, okay? I won't think less of you if you have to leave."

"Really?" he asked.

She kissed him on the cheek. "Really."

Xander waited while Anya dug through her bag for the keys to the Magic Box. He felt a little awkward being alone with her, especially since she'd been trying to have sex with him all day. Before this apocalypse they hadn't had a proper conversation in weeks, if not months. He wasn't sure what he should be doing with her now. He only knew he had to keep her away from Willow if he could. Anya wasn't taking it too well that she had been judged wicked and Willow hadn't.

But of course if you had to put Willow in the good pile or the evil pile, she went with the goodies. Everyone knew that. She'd gone a little crazy with grief when Tara died, but she wasn't *evil*. Of course, Xander didn't think Anya was particularly evil either. But she'd chosen to become a vengeance demon again, and he could understand how that would qualify her as wicked, at least to the untrained eye.

"Here it is," she said, unlocking the door of the shop. She stepped inside and immediately began coughing at the cloud of dust that greeted them. Xander pulled his T-shirt up over his mouth and breathed through the fabric.

"Where's the fire pot?" he asked. The place was a disaster. He wanted to get what they needed and get out of there as soon as possible.

"I don't know," Anya muttered. "I'm looking for hog turds."

"What?" Xander cried, but Anya had already disappeared into the dark interior of the shop. "Anya!"

She didn't answer. He took a deep breath and plunged in after her. He immediately fell over a hunk of twisted metal on the ground.

"I think they were downstairs," Anya called from farther inside.

Xander climbed to his feet and made his way to the front of the store. He turned—and stopped, shocked. The shop looked like a war zone. Shattered glass lay everywhere. The display cases had been upended and tossed around the room like toys. Plaster torn from the walls and ceilings lay strewn haphazardly about, amidst broken pieces of crystal and ceramic and the shredded remnants of books and tarot cards. Xander pulled his eyes from the wreckage to Anya, who was digging for yet another key to open the door to the basement storeroom.

"I thought you were going to clean up in here," he said.

Anya glared at him. "I did." She unlocked the door and vanished down the stairs.

Xander was almost afraid to step any farther into the room. The mess made him feel physically ill. He hadn't been here since Willow had trashed the place. He knew that the Magic Box was closed, of course, but in his mind it was always just as it had been when Giles and Anya still owned it. Perfect, comforting, like a second home to all of them. He never pictured it this way, devastated by Willow's battle with Buffy and Giles. He didn't want to be here.

"Ahn, let's go," he called. "We just need the fire pot."

Anya appeared at the top of the stairs. "I know I had hog turds here. All Willow had to do was ask me."

"She knows the store is closed," he said. "I'm sure it didn't even occur to her that you'd have leftover stock to give her."

"*Give* her?" Anya said. "I would've sold it to her at a high markup. Look what she did to my business! At least she should have the decency to buy up whatever I had left." She turned on her heel and headed back to the storeroom.

Xander had to admit that Anya had a point. He was positive that the only reason Willow hadn't offered to help Anya out was because it hadn't occurred to her. She'd been overwhelmed, trying to deal with her own magickal addiction and with her grief for Tara. They'd all been overwhelmed, in fact. They weren't in the best shape to deal with an apocalypse, let alone *the* apocalypse.

Xander picked his way through the rubble to the cash register. He sank down on the stool behind it and surveyed the room. There were little piles of rubbish here and there, and different bundles of herbs and other magick supplies that appeared still usable. Anya clearly had cleaned up in here, working her way through to find whatever she could salvage. *And it's still this bad?* he thought in disbelief.

An image of Willow at the Temple of Proserpexa flashed through his mind, her eyes black and inhuman, the veins on her face pulsing with dark magick. Xander shook his head to clear the memory, but this time it stayed with him. He'd been pushing away those thoughts of Willow ever since it happened. She'd gone to England with Giles, and Xander had gotten busy repressing his memories. He knew all the facts, of course. He knew everything that had happened, all the awful things she'd done under the influence of black magick, but somehow he'd managed to suppress the memory of the details—the way Anya's shop had been ruined, the way Warren's skin had been stripped from his body.

Xander retched as the image came back to him. How had this happened to Willow? Sweet little Willow, his best friend forever? She'd become a monster.

No wonder she's scared to do the Belial siphon spell, he thought. *She's afraid she'll turn back into that creature who wreaked such havoc here.*

Xander gasped as the truth of that hit him. She was afraid she'd lose her humanity again, and maybe she was right to be afraid. Look how bad it had been last time! Maybe she wasn't strong enough to keep it from happening again. The only thing that had saved her then was Xander. Their friendship had restored her humanity when she most needed it.

He leapt off the stool, knocking it over in his haste to get out of there. Willow was doing a discovery spell at this very moment. She needed him there to ground her. He had to get home before it was too late.

"Maybe if we sneak around to the kitchen door, we can get in without his knowing we're here," Buffy murmured. She and Spike were trying to hide behind the bushes that lined the windows of the dining hall, but it was kind of hard to do since the bushes were brown and withered. It was like trying to hide behind a pile of twigs.

"Isn't he supposed to know everything?" Spike asked.

"I think he's too busy to bother keeping tabs on

us," Buffy replied. She wasn't sure why she was hiding, really. She wanted to find a way to stall Michael, and the best way she could think of involved engaging him in yet another long conversation. He seemed to like nothing better than just chatting while the world fell down around them. Maybe if she got him talking, he'd forget to break another one of his bowls. But hiding from him wasn't going to help her accomplish that.

Still, she stayed where she was. Partially it was for Spike's sake, so he'd feel he was helping her. She knew he wouldn't be able to tolerate being any closer to Michael. But there was more to it than that. Buffy didn't feel like approaching the angel just yet. She knew she'd feel all calm and happy when she was with him, and right now the idea of that pissed her off. She wanted to hold on to the anger she felt toward Michael for what he was doing.

"All right, let's head around back," Spike said. He took off, crouching low to stay out of sight of the windows. Buffy took one last look inside. Something was happening. She inched closer to the glass to watch. The glowing zombies surrounding Michael had turned to face her. *Uh-oh,* Buffy thought. Suddenly they moved apart, creating an aisle of light straight from Buffy to Michael. He was looking straight at her, a gentle smile on his face.

"Hi, Buffy," he said. "Why don't you come inside?"

Busted. Buffy got up and headed for the glass double doors. The glowing zombies rearranged themselves so that her aisle to Michael remained in front of her. Intellectually Buffy knew these were the good guys, but she found the whole thing a little creepy. She walked slowly up the glowing aisle to Michael.

"Hey," she said. "How long did you know I was out there?"

"The whole time," he told her. "I thought you might be more comfortable in here." He gestured to a low table between two couches. "This was your favorite table when you went to school here, right?"

Buffy nodded, plopping down onto one of the overstuffed couches. "I used to take naps here in between my boring math for dummies class and even more boring theories of civilization class."

Michael sank onto the couch opposite her. "Are you ever sad that you left college?" he asked.

He always sounded genuinely interested when he asked her a question. *Remember why you're here,* she reminded herself. *You need to buy Willow some time.* "I had no choice. I had to take care of Dawn," she said. "And I wasn't sad, because I always thought I'd finish college later. I didn't know the world was going to end."

"Sorry," Michael said. "I'm sure a lot of people feel that way about things they couldn't finish."

"Well, couldn't you just slow things down, then?" Buffy asked. "You know, let the apocalypse slide for a year or two? I could finish school. You could, I don't know, start a rock band, see the country from your tour bus."

He chuckled. "I don't think so."

"But why not?" she pressed. "I mean, I know you

have to start the end time when you get the sign, but it's not like there's a deadline or anything. Is there?"

"There's no reason for delay," he said. "Once the sign is given, the end is already at hand. In fact, I have something to do right now." He lifted yet another clay bowl from his lap. Buffy hadn't seen it appear. It was a deep, wet, shiny red, and almost perfectly round, with an opening like a tiny pursed mouth at the top.

"What's in that one?" she asked.

"I don't know yet," he answered, staring down at the bowl.

"Can't you just wait an hour?" Buffy asked anxiously. "Let's talk about . . . about my lack of education some more."

Michael ignored her. He broke the bowl easily, a low wail escaping it, and laid the shards on the low table. Immediately Buffy leapt to her feet and dropped into a fighting stance. She didn't know what it would be this time, but she was hoping it would be an easy kill.

Nothing happened.

Buffy scanned the dining hall, waiting for the roof to collapse or the soda machine to turn into a giant mosquito. Or anything to happen at all.

"You can sit down," Michael said.

"Where's the big scary?" she asked suspiciously.

"It's pestilence," he told her. "I know as soon as it breaks."

Warily Buffy sat back down on the couch. "Meaning?"

"Boils," Michael said. "The wicked will be covered with boils."

"Oh. Ouch." *Poor Spike,* Buffy thought. She'd left him outside all alone and now he was going to be boil filled. She heard a sharp cry outside and turned to look. Two frat guys stood in the middle of the lawn, shrieking and scratching themselves. "Itchy boils," she said.

"Yeah," Michael agreed.

Spike streaked across the brown grass as if he were trying to outrun the pestilence. Every now and then he swatted at himself to make the itching stop. Michael shrugged apologetically.

"Are you the one who decides who's good and who's bad?" she asked.

"No," he replied. "I just break the bowls."

Buffy sighed and looked back at the wicked boil-marked fraternity boys. So far her plan to delay Michael really wasn't working at all. She hoped Willow discovered the Belial siphon spell soon.

The flashlight beam flickered. "Stop that," Anya said, shaking the light. She wasn't sure how old the batteries were; it was the emergency light that she'd always kept in the storeroom just in case. But there was no denying it—the light was fading fast. Frustrated, she blew a strand of hair off her forehead. She should've thought to bring another flashlight along.

"Stupid hog turds aren't here anyway," she muttered, casting a glance over the disheveled storeroom. This room hadn't been hit as hard as the main showroom, so things were mostly in their places. She'd been slowly carting stuff out whenever she could find a buyer for it. "Xander, do you have a flashlight?" she called upstairs. He didn't answer. With a sigh Anya grabbed the last fire pot off a shelf. Then she switched off the dying light and stomped back up to the main room.

Xander was gone.

She stood still for a moment, looking around in disbelief. He was gone. He'd left her here without even bothering to say good-bye. He'd abandoned her. Again.

Anya hurled the fire pot across the room, furious. Here she'd been all mopey about maybe never seeing Xander again, about dying without making love to him one last time. She'd been fussing over him all day. She'd only come here to help him and his friends try to save the world. But why was she even bothering? He didn't care. He didn't want to make love. He didn't even want to help her search through the Magic Box.

She wanted to be angry. She wanted to stay furious at him. But all she really felt was sad. An enormous lake of grief filled her mind, and she was afraid she might drown in it. Why didn't Xander love her anymore? Why would he leave her alone right in the middle of the apocalypse? He should want to spend this time with her as much as she wanted to be with him. Swallowing her feelings, she walked slowly across the room and picked up the fire pot. The impact with the wall had broken the edge, and a fine crack ran all the way through the stone.

Anya felt tears prick the backs of her eyes. No hog turds to make Willow feel guilty. A broken fire pot. And no Xander. Would things ever stop getting worse?

Fiery pain pierced her leg. "Ow!" she cried, bending to examine it. Then another pain on her arm. One on her forehead. More stabbing pains, one by one, burst out all over her body. First came the pain. Then, when it faded, unbearable itchiness took its place. Anya stumbled over to the window to look at herself in the light. She was covered with pimples. Only they were huge, pus-filled, itchy pimples, and they were everywhere. What was going on?

Outside on the street a woman was screaming and scratching herself. She was covered in the giant pimples just like Anya. *It's a plague,* Anya realized. *A curse on the wicked.* She sank to the floor underneath the window and hugged her knees to her chest. As if being left by the one man she loved wasn't enough to remind her that she was a loser, now Buffy's precious angel had sent a plague to make it clear to everyone. Anya slowly let herself fall sideways until she lay on the floor of her ruined shop, curled into the fetal position.

I'll just stay here, she decided. There was no point in going back to Buffy's house with everyone else. Xander clearly didn't care if he saw her again, and the others only tolerated her because of him. They tried to be nice, but she could tell how they really felt. She didn't want them all feeling sorry for her because of the itchy pimples.

The end would come soon. Well, soonish, anyway. She didn't think Willow would really be able to pull off the Belial siphon. Michael's apocalypse would come and the world would end. She could wait it out alone. She was used to being alone, and it would be nice to die here, in the only place she'd ever felt needed and important as a human.

The itching made her feel like her flesh was on fire. No amount of scratching would make it feel better. Anya closed her eyes and thought about her wedding. It was how she usually got herself to fall asleep when she was having trouble. She pictured it in every detail—the flowers, her perfect dress, Xander in his tux. She knew where every guest had been seated, and she imagined walking down the aisle past them all. Xander was waiting at the end, beaming at her, his expression filled with love.

Her eyes snapped open. It wouldn't work now. She didn't feel comforted by the daydream this time, she just felt angry. She couldn't believe Xander had done it again. How many times was she going to let him leave her? Her gaze fell on a pile of yellowing papers under the front door. *It must be mail I never noticed,* she thought absently. It had taken the post office a few weeks to stop delivering the mail after Willow's meltdown.

The itching from her giant pimples was driving her nuts. She sat up and reached for the mail to distract herself. Maybe there was money in one of the envelopes. There was still a deficit in her accounts receivable column. The pile of papers was stiff with age and dust and water—rain had probably seeped in under the door at some point. Two of the envelopes were stuck together. She carefully pried them apart, and a small white postcard fluttered out from in between them.

Anya scooped it up and squinted at the blurred ink on the card. It was a postcard from one of her suppliers in Utah—a recall notice. Anya scanned through the standard apology paragraph to see which product had been faulty.

Her breath caught in her throat as she saw the words: "Hog Turds Recalled. Final Notice. Defective. DO NOT USE."

CHAPTER THIRTEEN

Willow sat cross-legged on the living-room rug at the top point of the triangle she'd formed with yew branches. The other two corners were taken by Giles, who looked distinctly uncomfortable sitting on the floor, and Dawn.

A waste of space, her mind whispered. *They're useless. No power at all.*

She opened her eyes, shocked at her own thoughts. Dawn and Giles looked back at her blankly. Well, at least she hadn't said that out loud. She gave them a small smile and closed her eyes again. She'd been midway through the discovery spell when the strange thought interrupted her. If she didn't stay in the proper head-space, she'd have to start all over again.

The magic coursed around the triangle, winding its way through the branches. Willow controlled it from her spot. The plan had been that she would only take strength from the other two if she really needed it. She knew the main reason they were here was to make her feel safer. If the magick suddenly turned dark, they'd be able to pull her out of it.

Fools. They don't have the skill to do anything like that.

This time she didn't open her eyes. She knew where the thoughts were coming from. She could feel the thread of darkness within the magick. It wasn't overwhelming. It wasn't even unusual. She'd called on the goddess to teach her the strongest spell ever created; it was only natural that such a spell would use dark magick along with light. A year ago she wouldn't have thought anything of it, but now things were different. Now she could feel the seductive power of that darkness calling to her, tempting her with the memory of how invincible the dark magick had made her.

They don't understand me. They want to rein in my magick, force me to use only the weaker channels.

The thread of darkness grew stronger, pulsing through the yew branches like thick red blood. The discovery spell would work faster if Willow just gave in to the darkness, let it take over the whole spell. *Why not?* she thought. *Time is of the essence. Why not use the most powerful avenue at my disposal?*

The thread of darkness became thicker, almost pushing out all the light magick running through the triangle. Words began to form in Willow's mind, and images. The Belial siphon spell was coming to her now, fast . . . faster.

Willow relaxed into the stream of darkness, opening her mind to the knowledge of the spell. The dark power rushed like a drug through her body, awakening her senses. She gasped with pleasure.

"Willow!" Dawn's voice broke into her consciousness. "Are you okay?"

"Don't interrupt my concentration, idiot!" Willow snapped. She didn't open her eyes to see Dawn's reaction—she knew what it would be. Tears. As usual.

But the nasty thoughts felt wrong now, as if they came from something outside Willow. The thread of darkness began to shrink. The words of the Belial siphon came slower, until Willow felt as if she were receiving the information at half speed. She kept her focus on the spell, waiting until she had the whole thing in her mind.

Then she opened her eyes. Giles and Dawn were staring at her, worry etched on their faces. "Download complete," Willow joked. She toppled over onto the rug, exhausted. That discovery spell had taken a lot from her. Giles studied her, his brow wrinkled. "Why didn't you borrow strength from us?" he asked.

"I didn't need to," Willow said, still breathing hard. "I was afraid to expose you guys to the dark magick." She lifted her head to look at Dawn. "Dawnie, I'm so sorry. I didn't mean it."

Dawn stood up silently and walked away. Willow didn't blame her.

"Are you all right?" Giles asked.

"I will be," Willow replied. Wearily she heaved herself up to a sitting position. The weakness was passing, but in its place was a new dread. That had only been the discovery spell, and yet for a moment she'd succumbed to the darkness. How could she hope to work the Belial siphon spell without losing herself entirely? "I need to be alone," she told Giles. She climbed shakily to her feet and went upstairs to her room.

Willow dove into bed, pulled the covers over her head, and let the tears come. She couldn't do this! Even with the world at stake, she couldn't step up and help. If she tried to work the Belial siphon spell, she might very well turn into a monster and end the world herself in some unnatural way that would hurt everyone she loved. How had this happened to her? She used to love magick, and now it made her sick with fear. She hugged the pillow against herself and sobbed.

"Oh, come on now, it's not like the world is ending." Xander's voice startled her. "Oh, wait, yes it is."

Despite herself, Willow smiled. She pulled the blanket down and looked at her best friend standing in the doorway. "Don't make fun of me," she said, wiping tears from her cheeks.

"What, you mean because you're crying like a baby?" he asked. "I would never make fun of you for being such a wuss."

Willow chucked her pillow at him. Xander caught it and carried it back to the bed. He sat on the edge and looked at her, serious now. "You okay?"

"I was mean to Dawn."

Xander winced. "That's gotta hurt."

Willow nodded. "I know, of all the people to turn nasty on. Poor little Dawnie. I said I was sorry, but I don't think she understands."

"It was the magick making you all inhuman again," Xander guessed.

"Yeah." Willow felt perilously close to tears again, but she fought them back. "I gave in to it for a minute. It made the spell work faster."

"And it made you mean to Dawn," Xander said, "which I think she probably does understand, by the way."

"Maybe," Willow said doubtfully. "But I've hurt her so much because of my magick problem. I don't know if she can really forgive me."

"Don't sweat it. Dawn loves you," Xander said. "We all love you."

Willow narrowed her eyes and really looked at him. She hadn't noticed it at first, but Xander was spooked by something. "What's up?" she asked.

"I came to be with you," he said. "I know I was trying to help you ease back into the magick, but I don't think I really understood what you were afraid of. Now I do."

"What do you mean?" Willow asked.

"I had kind of blocked out the memory of you with the dark magick," he admitted. "I wouldn't let myself think about it after you left for England. I think I wanted to pretend that it was an aberration, not really you. That it was just a bad couple of minutes and you'd be able to get over it with a little effort."

Willow looked down at her pale hands, knotted together in her lap. If only it were that easy.

"But today I realized that it's not an aberration," Xander said. "It's really you. All that darkness is inside of you. It's part of who you are."

She nodded. "I don't want it to take over the rest of who I am," she whispered. "It did that once. I don't think I can survive a second time."

"I don't know if any of us can survive a second time," Xander said wryly.

Willow forced herself to meet his eye. "I don't think I can work the big undo spell," she said. "I know everyone's counting on me, but I just don't think it's possible. I'll turn into Queen Bitch again and I can't control what she does."

Xander took her hand. "That's why I'm here," he said. "I was with you last time you were Queen Bitch, so I know I can take her."

Willow's lips twisted in a grin. "Oh yeah?"

"Yeah," he said. "I'm serious, Will. I'm with you. We're going to do the Belial siphon spell together, and I'll keep you grounded. I'll sit in the circle and chant or dance around naked or whatever you need. And if you feel yourself slipping, you just latch on to me."

Willow clung to his hand, remembering how he'd pulled her back from the brink of self-destruction at the Temple of Proserpexa. The coven in England had taught her some methods of self-control. Between those and Xander, maybe she'd be okay. Maybe.

"I'll try," she said. "I'll do my best."

"That's my girl." Xander leaned forward for a hug,

and Willow buried her face in his sweatshirt. "Do you know the spell now?" he asked.

Willow nodded.

"Then let's get busy," Xander said. He pulled away but kept a hold on her arms. "You ready?"

Willow thought about it. She'd almost destroyed the world once. Now she had to help save it. She looked up at her best friend. "I'm ready," she said.

"You really drew the short angel straw," Buffy said thoughtfully. She and Michael had moved to the roof of the dining hall, and now they sat looking out over the once-beautiful campus. The glowing zombies milled about on the ground below. Buffy couldn't see Spike, but she had a feeling he was down there somewhere too, keeping an eye on her.

"What do you mean?" Michael asked.

"Well, you're an angel, right?"

"In a sense," he said. "I'm called by many different names. 'Angel' is the easiest term for you to understand."

"And angels are supposed to help people," Buffy went on. "You know, look out for their welfare." She was hoping to distract him from the clay bowl he held in his lap. This one was a mass of needlelike spikes. It had the same effect on Buffy as a loaded gun. It was a giant threat in the lap of an angel. She had no idea how long Willow needed to get her big undo spell ready. She just knew she needed to buy time, and that meant avoiding any more broken bowls.

"Some angels have that job," Michael said.

"Right, but your job is to kill everyone," Buffy said. "For an angel, that's gotta suck. You got the worst job."

Michael was silent for a moment. When he finally spoke, his voice was sad. "It takes a strong angel to do what I have to do," he said.

"It would take a strong angel to refuse to do what you think you have to do," Buffy pointed out.

"You don't get it, Buffy," he told her. "You see this ending as a bad thing. It isn't. I'm not trying to hurt anybody."

"But you are hurting them," she said. "How do you feel about that?"

"I serve the greater good," he said.

"So do I. But sometimes I get to see the faces of the people I save. I get to see who I make the sacrifices for. Sometimes," Buffy told him.

Michael didn't respond, so she tried a different angle. "It's probably a pretty senior-level job, though, ending the world. Bet you have a lot of perks."

Michael's face grew sad. "No. It's been lonely. And now that I'm finally free in the world, I have to bring it to an end. I never even got to live in the world or enjoy its beauty."

"Really?" Buffy asked, surprised. "Why not?"

"I've been asleep," he said. "Remember? The wolf in sheep's clothing woke me."

"Oh." Buffy frowned. "I thought that was just a euphemism."

"No, I was sleeping," he said. "For thousands and thousands of years. I've been asleep since the beginning."

That didn't make sense, Buffy thought. Michael had known who she was since the first time he saw her. "Then how do you know so much about me and my life?" she asked. "I assumed you were floating around and spying on me the whole time."

"My sleep isn't like the sleep of a human," he explained. "I was inactive, but I dreamed of the world and those within it. I couldn't live in the world, but I could watch it. I watched you. You were beautiful."

Buffy blushed, embarrassed. "I didn't think angels cared about stuff like that," she said.

Michael nodded gravely. "You were a force of light in the darkness," he told her. "Fighting with passion even when there was no hope to bolster you. You inspired me."

Buffy was speechless. "I—I just did what I had to do," she stammered.

"Not many would have fought so hard for so long," he told her. "You were a protector of the people. You were a hero."

She was silent, taking this in. It was pretty cool to know that she'd inspired an angel. But she realized that both of them had been referring to her in the past tense. As if she were already gone.

Michael stood.

"What's going on?" Buffy asked.

"It's time," he said, and he threw the clay bowl down onto the rooftop.

Xander watched Willow draw a magick circle on her bedroom floor with chalk. He was trying to radiate serenity to keep Willow calm, but instead he just felt extraneous.

"So that's the big bad Belial siphon?" he asked. "We just redo the little levitation spell?"

"No, we set up the spell the same way, but I use a different incantation," Willow explained. "That way the Belial siphon spell knows what I want it to undo. The levitation spell."

"But I thought the Belial spell would just undo whatever it wanted," Xander said.

"Maybe it will. But we're going to try to get it to just undo the levitation-wolf mess we made," Willow replied. "We need the hog turds again. I think I left them downstairs."

A sarcastic reply sprang to mind, but Xander bit it back. "I'll get them," he offered.

Willow smiled at him. "Thanks."

In the living room he found Dawn and Giles sitting on the couch. Dawn forced a smile when she saw him, but he could tell she was still upset about Willow snapping at her. "You okay, D-girl?" he asked.

She shrugged. "I just want this whole thing over with," she said. "One way or the other."

"Is Willow almost ready?" Giles asked.

"Yep. Just need some oinker dung to make the party complete," he replied, grabbing the glass pot of hog turds from the mantel.

The front door swung open and Spike rushed in. He scanned the room and ran straight to Giles. "What is this?" he demanded, slapping at his arms and face. "What's on me?"

Xander stared at the giant pus-covered red bumps that snaked up Spike's arms to his neck and face. Dawn recoiled with a little shriek.

"They itch!" Spike roared. "What are they?"

"Good question," Xander said, wrinkling his nose. Whatever they were, they also kind of smelled like cheese.

"Boils, I'd say," Giles replied calmly.

Spike scratched at his face. "Why?" he demanded.

"It's another stage of the apocalypse," Giles explained. "In many mythologies there is a series of plagues that affect only the wicked. Boils is a popular one."

"Well, that's very bloody special," Spike muttered. "If anyone needs me, I'll be in the bath." He stomped up the stairs.

"Hmm," Giles said. "I guess even the apocalypse has a silver lining."

Dawn giggled, but Xander stood rooted in horror. The wicked would be covered with boils. In their group that meant Spike and Anya. Anya must have those things too. She'd be itchy and tortured and humiliated, wherever she was. Xander groaned. He'd left her at the Magic Box. He'd just abandoned her there. In his haste to help Willow, he hadn't thought about Anya even once.

"What's wrong?" Dawn asked him.

"Anya," he said. "We went to get a fire pot from the Magic Box, but she insisted on looking for hog turds . . . so I left her there." He winced. "She was downstairs. She probably didn't even hear me leave."

Dawn shook her head, disappointed in him. "How could you do that?" she asked. "Don't you think Anya is a little sensitive when it comes to your deserting her?"

Xander hung his head. None of his female friends had ever entirely forgiven him for leaving Anya at the altar. "I wasn't thinking," he said. "I knew in my gut Willow needed me for the spell she was doing, and I bolted. I'm a schmuck. It's partly my fault she went back to being a vengeance demon at all. I'm a terrible person. Poor Anya, left alone with all those boils."

"Don't worry, I'm used to it," Anya snapped. She stalked through the front door with her head held high. "Here's your stupid fire pot." She flung a chipped stone bowl onto the coffee table.

"Oh!" Giles said, peering at it over his glasses. "I forgot about that. Um . . . turns out we don't need it for the Belial siphon after all."

Anya's eyes filled with rage.

"Sorry," Giles added. Then he got up from the couch and fled into the kitchen. Anya turned her glare on Xander.

"Um . . . how are you feeling?" Xander asked, trying not to stare at the hideous welts all over her skin.

"I feel just dandy," she said. "I love being covered in painful, itchy, ugly zits. Why do you ask?"

Xander sighed. She was spitting mad at him, and he should probably just let her get her yelling over with. "I'm sorry, Ahn," he said. "I didn't mean to leave you flat."

Anya rolled her eyes. "Oh, save it," she said with

surprising calmness. "I only came to give you this." She held out a small white postcard. Xander took it and tried to make out the smeared words.

"It's a recall notice," Anya said smugly. "For hog turds. There was a bad bunch going around for a while, and they recalled it. I already sent mine back. That's why I couldn't find any in the storeroom."

Xander squinted at the postcard. Bad hog turds? His brain was spinning. It couldn't be possible. . . .

"But Phillippa and her dumb house of enchantment didn't bother returning theirs," Anya went on. "So when Willow decided to buy from her, she got defective merchandise."

"You mean that's why our levitation spell went wrong?" Xander asked.

Anya gave him a tight smile. "That's right," she said. "You started the apocalypse because of a bad batch of pig poop. Nice going." Without another word she turned and walked out, slamming the door behind her.

Buffy stared at the broken bowl on the rooftop. The ceramic shards lay scattered about, some of them already crumbling into dust. Nothing else was happening. "Is this more pestilence?" she asked Michael.

"Nope." He stared at the bowl too. "This one just takes awhile to get going."

She took a step back, reaching into her jacket for a stake. She knew she probably couldn't fight it, and she knew it was almost definitely not a vampire. But it just made her feel better to have a weapon in her hand.

"Here it comes," Michael said.

"Where?" All Buffy could see was a fly sitting on one of the ceramic pieces. It rose into the air, buzzing. It wasn't a fly, it was a bee, Buffy realized. And there was a second one now. And a third. She drew back. A fourth bee appeared. A fifth.

She turned to Michael. "Bees?"

"Swarms," he said, nodding toward the ground around the dining hall below them. Buffy peered over the edge of the roof. A rat ran from the dining hall door. Then another and another. Soon there were hundreds of them pouring out onto the sidewalk. "Uck," Buffy said, revolted. "I always knew this place was a health code violation."

She turned back to Michael, but she could no longer see him. The bees had been multiplying faster and faster, and there was now a tornado of them spinning up from the shard of ceramic on the rooftop. The small black bodies flew furiously around in circles, practically blinding her. She couldn't see Michael. When she turned the other way, the bees were there too. She was surrounded, enclosed in a whirlwind of angry bees. She looked up, but the sky was dark with flying insects. There was no way out.

Buffy dropped the stake and covered her face. "Help!" she cried. "Michael, help!" She could feel the bees smacking into her, tangling in her hair. The buzzing was as loud as the drone of an airplane. Buffy closed her eyes and waited for the stinging to begin.

"Buffy!" Michael grabbed her hands and pried them away from her face.

"No!" she cried, fighting him. "They'll sting my eyes."

"They can't," he said, hugging her to him. "You're okay, Buffy. You're all right. Nothing can touch you. Look."

She forced her eyes open and looked. The bees surrounded them, a tornado made up of millions of flying bodies. Bees on all sides, a hundred thick. Bees up as far into the sky as she could see, but not one of them was flying at her. At worst, they brushed against her as they circled.

"They can't hurt you," Michael said, still holding her. "Do you understand? None of this will hurt you."

Buffy gazed at his beautiful face, so untroubled even in the midst of this nightmare twister. "Why not?" she asked.

He pushed a strand of hair off her face. "Because you're the Chosen One. Haven't you ever thought about what that means?"

"Yes," Buffy said. "It means I'm a hunter and a killer of evil things. It means I don't get to be normal."

"It means you're one of the greatest forces of good in the world," Michael said gently. "Buffy, you're a kind of angel too. You were chosen to do a job and you've done it superbly. Your job is done now, but you are still the Chosen One. Nothing that will happen in this apocalypse will harm you. You are protected."

Buffy stared around at the swarm of bees. The tornado was expanding outward, widening the clear center where they stood. Soon, she knew, bees would begin to fling themselves out in every direction, thousands of bees swarming everywhere. But the area around them seemed to have its own invisible force field. Buffy stared up at Michael.

"You mean I'm like you?" she asked. "That . . . that thing around you. The force field that keeps me from fighting with you. Do I have one of those too?"

"In a way," he said. "You cannot be harmed by plagues that target the wicked. Or by anything that will happen. If you want, you can stay with me and observe it right up until the end."

The words hit Buffy hard. The end. She was supposed to be slowing things down and she'd forgotten! She'd been so distracted by Michael's compliments that she'd forgotten why she was here with him. She was here to fight him. She might be a force of good just like he was, but that didn't mean she agreed with what he was doing. Somehow she would find a way to stop him, no matter what it took.

She looked him in the eye. "I will," she said. "I'll stay until the end."

CHAPTER FOURTEEN

"I think we're ready," Xander called.

"Finally," Dawn said. She leapt up and charged upstairs, but Giles stayed where he was on the living-room couch. He looked at the fire pot Anya had brought from the Magic Box and sighed. He remembered ordering this fire pot; it had been before he moved back to England. At the time the most complicated decision had been about his responsibilities to Buffy—should he stay and play the parent figure, or should he leave her to grow up on her own?

It had been a hard choice at the time, but compared to the responsibilities facing them all right now, it seemed mind-numbingly simple.

"Giles?" Xander called down. "You coming?"

"In a minute," he replied. He didn't feel right about this spell, the Belial siphon. It wasn't entirely good magick. Of course, it wasn't thoroughly black magick either. It was a spell so old that it incorporated pieces of both the good and the bad. That was probably what made it so powerful. But should they use it? *Could* they use it?

On a whim Giles snatched a box of matches from the coffee table. He lit one and threw it into the fire pot. *"Flagrare,"* he said. The entire bowl burst into flame, a conflagration contained harmlessly inside the cool stone. Giles stared into the different colors flickering within the tongues of orange flame. When he was young and first learning about magick, he'd always used fire pots to help him meditate, but now the blaze wasn't helping him at all.

Should he stop Willow from attempting this spell? He wasn't convinced that she was strong enough to control it, especially not after what had happened during her discovery spell. He hated to think of her slipping back into the darkness of her magickal addiction.

But it was more than that. He was worried that they were overstepping their bounds. Michael really was some sort of messenger, or higher being, Giles believed. He was a force of good, and he was doing what was meant to be done. He was starting the true end time. Giles didn't want that time to be now. But who was he to decide? Who were any of them to think they knew better than Michael? In all his years as a watcher, Giles had never been called upon to fight a battle against another force of good. The group had made a decision to do so, but it didn't sit well with him.

The cast of the fire changed from a deep blue to a sickly greenish color. *What does that mean?* Giles wondered. Was it a warning? Or did it mean nothing? Maybe he was foolish for even worrying this much. If the world was meant to end now, then end it would—no matter what they did.

"Giles?"

He started, tearing his gaze away from the fire pot. Willow stood in front of him, her big eyes filled with worry. "Is there something wrong?" she asked.

Giles felt his fears melt away as he looked at her. Here he was worrying about the fate of the world when Willow was petrified of something much more immediate: the darkness in her own soul. He studied her, shocked to realize how tiny she still was—a small little girl with pale skin and a worried frown. Still so very young. He hadn't noticed that for a long time now. When he thought of Willow, he thought of her frightening power and of how dangerous she could be. He'd never known such a powerful witch in his life. His focus had been on helping her control the power. He'd forgotten that she was still just a girl, still afraid, still looking to him for guidance.

A sudden surge of resentment filled him, taking him by surprise. She was too young to die, too full of potential. They all were. He raised his eyes to see Xander and Dawn standing on the staircase, waiting for him to join them for the spell. He thought of

Buffy out there fighting, always fighting no matter what the odds. They deserved better than this. These young people had saved the world countless times. To have it taken away from them now was simply too cruel.

This is the true, predestined end time, Giles thought. *And I don't care.*

He smiled at Willow. "Are you ready?" he asked.

"I'm not sure," she admitted. "I am ready, but I'm scared."

A sound like rain caught his attention, and he looked up to see bees hitting the glass of the windows—thousands of bees. They didn't have much time. Giles put on his best librarian voice. "Nonsense," he told Willow. "You're a powerful witch. You just have to remember what the coven taught you. Your power comes from the earth and it contains all the light and dark of nature itself."

Willow nodded.

"The earth needs you now," he went on. "You'll connect to it and draw upon its strength for this spell. You've nothing to be afraid of."

"I'm afraid of losing myself," she said.

"If you start to lose yourself, Xander will pull you back," Giles said. He put a hand on her shoulder. "And if he can't, then I will."

Dawn left the stairs and came over to Willow's side. "And if Giles can't, then I will," she said softly.

Willow gave her a teary smile. "Aw, you guys," she said.

"Upstairs!" Giles commanded. "This is no time for sentiment." Willow hugged him anyway.

The angel's head lay on its side, half buried by dead leaves, its cracked marble face still wearing a cherubic smile. Michael bent to pick it up, brushing the dirt from its cheek.

Buffy looked around the courtyard. She hadn't been back since she killed the first wolf, so she hadn't been expecting the destruction. The entire fountain looked as if it had exploded from within. *I guess that's kind of what happened,* she thought. She'd asked Michael to bring her to his home, hoping the detour would delay him a bit. But she hadn't been expecting to come back here.

"So this was you?" she asked. "You were here the whole time?"

"Here and other places," he said. "This is where I woke up."

She ran her hand over a dark stain on the lip of the fountain—blood from the wolf she'd killed. "I know," she said. She smiled at him. "I wouldn't mind sleeping for a couple of thousand years. I'm kinda jealous."

"Well, time doesn't work the same way for me," Michael said. "And I wasn't here the whole time. Not physically. Space doesn't work the same way for me either."

"Did you see me with the wolf? The sheep-wolf?" Buffy asked.

He nodded.

It was strange, Buffy thought. She always felt so

alone when she was out patrolling, as if she were part of the night itself. But there had been an angel watching over her and she hadn't even known it. "I always liked this fountain," she said. "It made me feel safe. I guess now I know why."

When Michael didn't answer, she glanced over her shoulder to see what he was up to. To her horror, he was holding another clay bowl, this one unglazed, the sides uneven and rough. Buffy spun to face him. "Already?" she cried. "But you just broke the last one an hour ago."

"I know. But it's time," he said sadly.

Buffy stared at the bowl. How could such devastation come from something so small? She noticed that Michael's hands were shaking, and suddenly she felt sorry for him. Being the Slayer had been a hard job—lots of violence, lots of sacrifice—but his job was a million times harder. The stress must really be getting to him.

"How many more of these puppies do you have to break?" she asked.

"This is the last one," he said, keeping his eyes on the bowl as if it might suddenly leap up and bite him.

"The last bowl. Really?" she asked. "What's next? Cuisinarts?"

"No," Michael said. "This is it. After this my job is done."

Buffy stared at him, trying to understand. If his job was done, didn't that mean it was over? The apocalypse was finished? The world had ended? "But . . . but you said we had two days," she said stupidly. "That means there's a day left."

Michael's hands shook harder. He didn't answer.

"There's still a day left," Buffy said again. "You said so! You can't take our last day." She knew she sounded like a three-year-old throwing a temper tantrum, but she couldn't stop herself. She'd never felt so helpless in her life.

"The beast of the land emerges today," Michael explained. "It will take him a day to swallow the earth."

"To *swallow* it?"

He nodded. "That's how it ends."

Buffy decided to ignore that for now. "But we do have a day?" She felt an absurd relief, at least until Michael began shaking his head.

"This is the place," he said. "I break the bowl and the beast emerges here."

"Okay," Buffy said. "So?"

"So it begins devouring the earth right here," Michael said. He finally lifted his eyes from the bowl. They were brimming with tears. She'd never seen him express such sadness. It's because he cares about me, she realized. "Sunnydale goes first," Michael continued. "Today. Now."

Willow adjusted one of the white candles in the middle of the chalk circle on her bedroom floor. "Does this look right, Xan?"

Xander squinted at it. "Pretty much," he answered. "They were in a straight line."

"Pretty much is not acceptable," Giles reminded them. "Everything must be exactly as it was when you did the levitation spell."

"Which time?" Xander asked. "'Cause the first time, maybe it was a little to the right. . . ." The saliva dried up in his throat. He turned to Willow. She got it before he said another word.

"Oh, my god, that's right!" she cried. "We did the levitation spell two times! How could we not think of that?"

Dawn glanced from Giles to Willow, her eyes wide and worried.

Xander swallowed hard, working up enough spit to speak. "It's always somethin' when you're trying to save the world." He smiled at Dawn, and she smiled back. She was Buffy's sister, all right. He didn't doubt that she was frightened, but here she was, by their side, facing the end time bravely.

"Giles, what do you think?" Willow asked. "How will it know which one to undo? The first one is the one that started it all. But won't it automatically undo the more recent one, like the undo function on the computer?"

"There must have been some difference in the two spells," Giles answered. "No matter how small."

"Same candles, same ingredients," Willow said.

"Same participants," Giles muttered.

"There was a fly in the room the first time," Xander volunteered, proud of himself for remembering. "It tried to dive-bomb my eye. Does that count? And, I was wearing a different shirt. And, the power bolt went out the window the first time. And—"

"Xander, Xander, thank you," Giles cut him off, "but I was referring to the spell itself. To the words spoken, to the placement of the, er, hog feces, that sort of thing."

Xander felt his face flush. He'd thought some of that stuff was pretty good.

"Wouldn't Xander's moving his hand and throwing the power out the window be a difference?" Willow asked. Xander felt a little less stupid.

Giles shook his head. "The spell was complete at that point. Think, you two. Is there anything that differentiates the two spells themselves?"

Willow and Xander stared at each other. Willow shrugged helplessly. Xander shrugged back.

"Does this mean we can't do the siphon?" Dawn asked, her voice high with tension.

"No way," Xander told her. "We're going to do it. We'll just—" He thought for a second. "We'll just double the ingredients and undo both spells. Right, gang?"

Now Willow and Giles did the stare and shrug.

"Um, okay," Willow said.

"Yes, good plan," Giles agreed in a voice that meant the exact opposite.

"Great!" Xander said. "Let's do it."

A single perfect tear slid down Michael's beautiful cheek. But Buffy's eyes were dry; she knew what she had to do. Maybe Willow would get the undo spell right, but whether it worked or not, Buffy had to fight on her own. And fight she would, even if all the angels ever created came and cried in front of her the way Michael was doing.

"You know how you keep telling me my job is done?" she asked. "That I'm not the Slayer anymore?"

He nodded.

"Well, you're wrong," Buffy said. In one swift move she leapt toward him and kicked the thick bowl from his hands. Time seemed to slow as the rough clay bowl flew through the air.

I can't let it break, Buffy realized. She didn't know if Michael had to break it himself in order to release his earth beast, but she didn't want to take the chance. She dove for the bowl and caught it by the rim. She grabbed it as hard as she could, but it slipped away from her and tumbled to the ground.

Buffy held her breath, dreading the sound of it breaking, but it came to rest on a pile of leaves, unharmed.

"Buffy—," Michael started.

Afraid to let him get it, Buffy threw herself on top of the bowl as if it were a fumbled football. Instantly a searing pain shot through her body. The bowl was scalding hot. Buffy screamed. It felt as if she'd fallen into a pit of molten lava. The agony drove every thought from her mind; she couldn't even make herself move.

Michael grabbed her arm and hauled her off the bowl. The pain stopped, but she felt dizzy and weak.

"What were you thinking?" Michael yelled.

Buffy squinted up at him, trying to focus through the aftermath of the pain. She'd never seen him angry before. She hadn't even known he could get angry.

"So I can't fight you and I can't touch the bowl," she gasped. "Anything else I need to know?"

"When will you understand?" he said. "You can't stop it. No one can stop the end from coming. Not even me."

He picked up the bowl as if it were completely cool to the touch. His hands were no longer shaking as he held it aloft. "I'm sorry, Buffy," he said. Then he began to break the bowl in half.

Willow sat inside the magick circle on her bedroom floor. Xander sat opposite her, with the same thin notebook on the ground in between them. Giles and Dawn sat together on the bed, watching intently.

"Okay," Willow said. "Here we go." She lit the three white candles one by one, surprised at how calm she felt. When they were all burning, she nodded at Xander. He picked up the glass pot of hog turds, scooped out a handful, and spread it liberally on the cover of the notebook. He didn't even make a face, Willow noticed.

Xander wiped his palm on his jeans, then held out his hands. Willow grasped them and hung on tight. She locked her eyes on her best friend and took a deep breath. *Don't think about the consequences,* she told herself. *Just think about the spell.*

"We call on the elements of the universe," she said. "Fire. Water. Earth. Air. Remove the harm spoken by your servants." Her voice faltered a little as she felt the magick begin to stir within her. Xander squeezed her hands. She swallowed down her uneasiness and took a moment to steady herself.

"If we gave you the moon, you give us the sun. If

we gave you winter, you give us spring. If we gave you illness, you give us health. . . ."

The power was all throughout her body now, and spreading beyond her like roots digging deep into the ground and branches spreading high into the sky. Willow felt as if the words of the spell came from the earth itself as she continued.

"If we gave you blackness, you give us light. If we gave you death, you give us birth." She took a deep breath. "Remove the harm spoken by your servants."

Darkness was coming now, spreading through her body with the rest of the power. At first she wanted to shy away from it, but then she remembered Giles's words: "Your power comes from the earth and it contains all the light and dark of nature itself."

That's it, Willow realized. That was the key. The darkness was frightening, yes, but it was also necessary. The earth gave birth to both the dark magick and the white magick. Both on their own were strong, but together they were as strong as the earth itself.

I can't be afraid of the darkness, she thought. The darkness gave strength to the spell. She simply had to be strong enough to control the black magick, to not let it take over completely. Willow closed her eyes and concentrated on the touch of Xander's hands. He was her link. He would keep her grounded.

Then she opened herself up to the darkness.

"Michael, no!" Buffy yelled.

He hesitated, still holding the bowl aloft.

"Please don't," she begged.

"I have no choice," he said gently. "Buffy, you have nothing to fear. I promise."

"But I don't want to die," she told him. "I already know what that's like."

Michael lowered the bowl. "You died," he said. "So you should know that it's nothing to be afraid of."

"It was a wonderful place," Buffy agreed, "wherever I was. It was paradise."

"So why are you trying so hard to stop me?" he asked. "Why won't you stop fighting?"

"After I was brought back, it took me a long time to get over having died," she told him. "I thought I'd never want to live again. I spent months just trying to numb the pain of being ripped away from that perfect place."

"Then you should want to get back there," Michael said.

"But I don't," Buffy replied. "Not yet. That's what I learned, and it was the hardest lesson of my entire life. I learned that I want to live. That life is worthwhile, even when it really sucks. I want to see my little sister grow up."

"Dawn will be with you—"

"That's not enough!" Buffy cried. "I don't want her to die. She's only fifteen. I want her to grow up and go to college and . . . and whatever she wants to do. I want to see Willow fall in love again. I want to see Giles have a family. I want to see Xander start his own construction firm. I want to be happy." She stopped, her words caught in her throat. "I never had time to be happy."

"But you were happy when you died."

"I want to be happy here," she said. "I want the world to go on. All the good and bad stuff. For everyone."

"You're asking me to not do my job."

"It takes so long to figure things out here. We all need more time. Everybody. I want everybody to figure out what I did. And now that I have finally figured it out, I want a happy life. With a husband, and children, and a normal job. I want my life."

Buffy reached out and touched his hand. "I'm asking you to give me my life." He still held the bowl, but it no longer felt hot. "Please. This one time, don't do your job."

Michael stood frozen, as if the very idea of shirking his duty had stripped him of the ability to speak.

"Michael, it's up to you," she said. "You have a job, and you were chosen to do it. But ultimately it's your choice. You can decide."

"Have you ever not done your job, Buffy?" he asked. "Have you ever put aside being the Slayer? For anyone?"

Yes! She wanted to scream it. *Yes!* But it wasn't true, and she knew it.

"You killed Angel once," Michael said. "I watched you. I felt your pain. But you killed him because you had to."

"I had to save the world," she said. "Just like you do."

"No. You had to do your job," Michael replied. "Just like I do."

There was nothing else to say, and Buffy knew it. They were both bound to their fated roles. He would be the angel who ended the world, and she would be the Slayer. She stood on tiptoe and kissed him on the cheek.

"I'm truly sorry," Michael said.

Then he broke the last bowl.

CHAPTER FIFTEEN

Spike leaned his head back against the wall of the bathroom. He'd filled the tub with cold water and dumped in three of those oatmeal pouches Buffy used to soothe her sunburns and battle wounds, but the boils still itched like crazy. The sensation was so constant and intense that he could hardly think straight.

He wondered where Buffy was. Off with the angel, probably. Spike banged his head back against the wall a few times. He felt so useless. He'd wanted to help Buffy, to be with her until the end, and instead he was trapped in a bathtub. Even if he hadn't been attacked by the boils, he wouldn't have been of any use to her. He couldn't get within a block of that angel.

From down the hall came the sound of Willow's voice. She was saying an incantation, over and over. *I wonder if that's the big special undo spell,* he thought. He scrunched up his face, concentrating hard, trying to hear better. But he had no luck; it was too muffled to make out the words.

Giving up, Spike slipped beneath the oatmeal-filled water to soothe the welts on his face.

Under the water he thought things through. This could be his last moment on earth. At any second the individual-disaster portion of the apocalypse could come to a close and the true end could begin. Or, if Willow was working the Belial siphon, the fabric of reality could simply unravel. What if it undid his whole life? It really wouldn't be fair to lose his soul to an undo spell, especially when he'd had to fight so hard to get it. Or what if the spell undid everything way back to when he was still human? Would he make the same choices? Would he let Drusilla turn him into a vampire?

Spike sat up quickly, splashing gooey water all over. He didn't want any of those things to happen. He didn't want to change anything about his long life, because anything he changed would lead him away from Buffy. If he wasn't a vampire, he would've been dead for a hundred years before she was born. So it was worth it to have lived his life of evil, even though the memories tormented him now. It was worth it, because he'd gotten to love Buffy.

And now he might never see her again. Desperately Spike grabbed the bar of green herbal soap and used it to write on the tiled wall: "I love you." It was all he could do.

The two pieces of the broken bowl landed on the dirt at exactly the same time. Buffy felt the earth shift, moving as if someone had pulled a carpet out from under her feet. She stepped back hastily as the earth moved in toward the remains of the bowl. A small hill formed underneath the pieces of clay. The hill grew rapidly, pulling all the surrounding earth into itself—dirt, leaves, dead grass. The hill rose higher into the air as it sucked up land from deeper down, pulling up buried rocks, earthworms, and thick, wet mud.

Buffy scurried back again as the hill began to expand sideways at the same time, pulling in the earth from even farther away, creating a large circle of movement around itself. It sucked rapidly, digging down as it expanded. She wouldn't have anyplace to stand in a matter of minutes. The ground beneath her feet was moving like a treadmill. Buffy began to jog in place.

Michael took her arm and pulled her toward him, settling her on a small piece of ground that wasn't moving. "We'll be safe here," he said. He watched serenely as the hill continued to grow.

"What is that?" Buffy asked him.

"The beast of the earth," he replied calmly.

Buffy frowned. It didn't look like a beast to her. Although, now that she was able to watch without having to worry about keeping her balance, she began to notice some other things about the hill of dirt.

It seemed to be walking, for starters. It had formed two massive legs, or else it had simply split itself in two about halfway down. In fact, it seemed to have created arms, too. Or protrusions of earth, at least, reaching out to grab trees and pull them into itself. Before Buffy's eyes it had become a monster. With every step it took, it pulled down more of the surrounding earth, sucking it up and adding the dirt, grass, rocks, trees, plants, and unlucky creatures to its own body. It grew taller and wider every second, while the park around it was simply becoming a hole.

"That's how it devours," Buffy said. "It takes everything into itself. The whole world?"

"Yes," Michael said. "It will spend one day, and at the end there will be nothing left."

His voice was still sad, but it was also still calm. Buffy studied the angel next to her. He was watching the earth beast not with pride, but with resignation. His job was to oversee the beast, she realized. He had to stand here on his one safe spot of earth and watch until this monster had finished eating everything—and everyone—on the planet.

I could stay with him, she thought. He'd told her she was like him, a force for good. Special. Chosen. She would be allowed to stand here safely and watch as the world ended. She'd be spared the terror and the pain of the last moments. She'd be detached like Michael, sad about the method of the end but serene in the knowledge that it was all for the best.

The beast was fifteen feet tall now, and almost as wide. As Buffy watched, the monster devoured the stone angel head. The tiny piece of marble disappeared inside the mound of black, squirming earth.

"No," she said. "I won't let this happen."

Michael looked at her in surprise. "It's already happened," he said. "There's nothing you can do now."

"I can fight," she said. She leveled a challenging look at him. "And so can you."

"It's no use," he told her. "This can't be stopped."

"I've never met anything I can't stop," she said. "I'll fight it or I'll die trying. I won't stand here and think I'm above it all."

"Look at it, Buffy," Michael said, an edge of panic creeping into his voice. "How can you fight that?"

Buffy looked. He had a point, unfortunately. The beast was made of the substance of the earth itself. It had no eyes, no mouth, not even a real head. She couldn't find a single spot that would be vulnerable. Her courage flagged a tiny bit.

The monster was twenty feet tall. It had reached the concrete pathway that led through the woods to the angel fountain. It began pulling slabs of cement into itself, placing them at the ends of its arms. Now with every swing of an arm, the concrete smashed against trees, knocking them violently to the ground, splintering thick trunks as if they were tiny twigs.

"Stay with me," Michael said. "You can't fight it."

Buffy didn't need to see his beautiful face; she could picture the look of serene worry it wore. She was sick of Michael's resignation. She didn't even glance his way. "Watch me," she said.

She leapt off the small, solid patch of earth where

she stood with Michael. "No! I can't protect you from there!" he cried.

But she ran full force at the beast of the earth. Being a safe observer wasn't for her. The beast had no obvious weak spots, so she'd just have to hit it wherever she could. With all her strength Buffy swung her fist at it. She connected with the dirt and moss and wriggling worms—and her hand sunk right in.

Okay, so that didn't work, she thought, pulling her arm back. Her arm didn't move. Buffy pulled harder. Her arm remained sunk into the body of the beast. Frantic, she tried to plant her feet for leverage, but the earth underneath her was moving, being sucked up into the monster. "Give me back my arm, you giant mud pie," she shouted, using her other hand to dig at the quicksandlike dirt around her flesh.

The beast of the earth didn't respond. It was oblivious of her. It was oblivious of all the life it slurped up.

Buffy felt her feet lift off the ground as the monster grew taller. With every passing second more of her arm disappeared inside as its body expanded. She was dragged along with it, slowly being devoured. She twisted around to see Michael. He was watching her, horrified.

"I thought you said nothing could hurt me," she cried.

He didn't answer. He just stood still, his face a mask of anguish.

The monster gave a great heave, and Buffy's arm slid in up to her shoulder. Her body was now pressed against it, and she could feel the mud attaching to her hip and leg like more quicksand ready to pull her inside.

"Michael!" she screamed. "Help me!"

But he didn't move.

Anya was through scratching the bumps. It didn't help. When you scratched them, the itching just got more intense. She'd tried imagining a fiery vengeance upon each and every giant red boil, but it didn't help. Now she was just resigned to them.

The Magic Box was a mess. Looking around the health hazard of a store, she had to admit that Xander had been right about that. She'd cleaned it up some right after Willow destroyed it, but eventually she'd had to give up. It was too big a job. The board of health said the place couldn't be salvaged, and they were right. Since then she'd been running little search-and-rescue missions to find any useful stock left in the rubble.

But today she was going to clean it up for real. It was her store and she wasn't about to let the world end without putting her affairs in order.

The only broom she could find was missing half its handle. So Anya bent over, pushing the stiff bristles against the floor. She created a pile of plaster, dirt, and broken glass with every stroke. It wasn't fair. Willow had done this to her beloved shop, but Willow apparently wasn't wicked. But she, she who had lost her man and her business all in one spring, *she* was wicked!

In truth, Anya didn't think Willow was wicked.

Not really. Not like most of the demons she knew. Not like Glory had been, or the Mayor. She probably wasn't even as wicked as Anya herself, all things considered. But it didn't seem fair that Willow could coast by on her goodness just because she was a friend of the Slayer. Just because she was sorry for what she did. Anya was sorry too, sorry for a lot of things she'd done in her life.

"I'm sorry I ever fell in love with Xander," she muttered, sweeping another pile of grime into a corner. And she was sorry that she'd become a vengeance demon again. She wouldn't dare admit that one out loud, but secretly she was very, very sorry about that.

Ripping unfaithful men limb from limb just didn't have the same allure that it used to. Every time she exacted revenge for some jilted girl, all she could think of was Xander. And as angry as she was at him, as much as she wanted to hate him, she just couldn't stop loving him. She didn't want Xander to be turned inside out, or boiled in hot oil, or eaten by a horde of fire ants. None of her typical vengeance demon tricks would make her pain go away.

But Xander didn't love her. She stopped sweeping and looked around the shop. It was falling apart. It had been closed for months now. There was nothing left here for her. And Xander wasn't here. When she'd slammed out of Buffy's house earlier, he hadn't even followed her. It was over. Her life as a human was over. No more Xander, no more Magic Box, no more anything.

Anya let the broom drop to the floor. The world

was ending, and she was relieved. At least she wouldn't have to feel the pain of missing Xander anymore.

She walked out of the Magic Box. The sky was a deep, dark blue, peaceful even though the sun was gone. Off in the distance Anya heard a strange sound, as if rocks and buildings were falling. But right here everything was still. She locked the door of her store for the last time and let the key fall onto the sidewalk.

Then she turned her back on the Magic Box, and her memories of Xander, and walked toward the sounds of destruction.

"Remove the harm spoken by your servants," Willow said for the twenty-first time. Xander knew. He'd been keeping count.

His hands were sweaty—Willow had been holding on to them tightly ever since starting the spell. He was trying to stay alert, to pour out good vibes and healthy, regular-guy energy to help keep her grounded. But Willow's eyes had been closed the whole time, and even though he held her hands, he wasn't sure she even remembered he was there.

Xander glanced over at Giles and Dawn on the bed. They looked back at him silently. Did they feel what he felt? Their drawn faces told him they did. He—and they—felt nothing. No magick. No power, either dark or light, was coursing through Willow's body. The Belial siphon was supposed to be the strongest spell of all time. So where was the magick?

Then a hand slammed into Xander's chest. He gasped, winded, as the hand burned through his flesh and reached his heart. Squeezing, sucking, twisting. The life began to flow from him, his battered heart leaking it out through the hole in his chest.

He tried to jerk his hand away from Willow. He wanted to hold it over the hole, but Willow wouldn't let go. Still trying to breathe, he raised his eyes to Willow's face. She stared right at him. Her eyes were black.

She's using dark magick, he thought frantically. He needed to send her some humanity, to keep her from straying too far. But how? How could he do that with this hole in his chest?

He looked down at himself. Nothing was happening. There was no hole, no hand squeezing his heart. But now his vision was becoming dim, the edges of the room turning dark before his eyes.

It's Willow, he realized. She was drawing strength from him, pulling energy from his body and his soul to use in her spell. She would kill him.

Her black eyes stayed locked on to him. "So mote it be," she thundered.

Xander felt sick to his stomach; he was passing out. Willow let go of his hands. Instantly the air rushed back into his lungs, dizzying him. The tunnel vision began to clear. He was himself again, but as weak as a kitten. Willow's green eyes watched him, filled with worry.

The spell was done. Finished. He'd given her enough. He'd pulled her back. They sat in the magick circle, both breathing hard, the poo-smeared notebook between them. They waited.

Nothing happened.

Xander saw the hope slowly fade from Willow's eyes. He glanced up at the other two. Giles met his gaze for a moment and shook his head. Dawn began to cry.

The Belial siphon hadn't worked. They had failed.

Buffy couldn't feel her right arm. It had been inside the earth monster for so long that it had become numb. Her right leg was pretty much inside the mound of dirt now too. The body of the beast was expanding constantly, beginning to creep over her face. She twisted as far as she could, trying to keep her mouth and nose free of the mud.

Would she drown in this monster, or suffocate?

It had reached the end of the park by now, and Buffy could see the road. Soon they would be in downtown Sunnydale. Already the beast had been sucking up rabbits and skunks and other forest critters. When it reached the town, it would start to devour people. Most of the Sunnydale residents had been fleeing over the past few days, but Buffy knew it didn't matter. The beast of the earth would catch up to them eventually. There was no way to escape it.

She spat a twig out of her mouth. The thick, compacted mud was pressing against her chest and her back, squeezing her. She couldn't take a deep breath. Where was Michael?

Buffy squirmed around as much as she could, twisting her head to peer over her left shoulder. To her surprise, the angel was running alongside. He'd left his safe place. He had chosen not to observe the end. He was participating now, jogging next to the monster, watching Buffy get swallowed.

The monster switched its course slightly, allowing it to suck Buffy's left leg into its body. From where she was stuck, she could no longer see how big the beast was, but it must be ten feet taller than it had been when she punched it—she was now dangling high up in the air. The beast stepped onto a swing set, crushing the metal frame in a matter of seconds. The collapsed tubing clanged and groaned as it was sucked up into the monster.

Buffy was now waist deep in the beast. In less than a minute it would surround her entirely. She turned her eyes to Michael. He was still keeping pace with her, his features distorted with horror as he watched. She'd never seen so much emotion on his perfect face. With all her strength she stretched out her left arm as far as she could, her hand toward the angel.

"Michael," she croaked. "Please do something."

Determination filled his blue eyes. He jumped up and grabbed Buffy's hand, his strong fingers closing around her wrist. With a great heave he yanked Buffy from the monster's body. She felt the mud sucking at her, trying to hold her in. Branches and rocks scraped against her as she moved. But finally the quicksand released her with a loud slurping sound, and she fell into Michael's arms.

They both tumbled to the ground as the beast moved on, oblivious.

Buffy concentrated on breathing for a moment. She was filthy and slimy—and free! She turned to

Michael with a grin. "That wasn't part of your job," she said.

He smiled back nervously. "I know." He sounded a little frightened.

Buffy took his hand. "Thank you," she said. "I knew you'd come through for me."

"I don't know what will happen now," he told her. "What do we do?"

That must be the first time he'd ever asked the question. Buffy looked around. The ground beneath them was nothing but bare rock. Once, it had been a green field studded with wildflowers that ran along the main road into town. Now all of its earth had gone into the monster.

Has Willow done the spell yet? she wondered. She had no way of knowing, and no way of helping her friends. No way other than to keep doing what she was doing. She got to her feet.

"We fight," she told Michael. "Together."

"I don't think we can win," he said. "You know I can't call it back."

"That doesn't matter," Buffy replied. "We just have to try."

"That's what I wanted," Michael told her. "I wanted to try."

She sprinted to the front of the monster, trying to get ahead of it. Michael followed. "Ready?" Buffy asked him. He nodded.

She stopped running and turned to take a stand. Michael followed her lead. The beast of the earth moved toward them, unaware and unafraid of the

Slayer and the angel in its path. It reared up over them, thirty feet tall.

"This is it," Buffy whispered. Michael stepped closer, standing shoulder-to-shoulder with her to face the beast.

The beast lifted one massive leg. The size of it blotted out the sky as it moved down toward their heads. *It will cover us completely,* Buffy realized too late.

The monster reared over them, ready to step on them. Then it collapsed.

Buffy screamed as a massive quantity of mud splashed onto her, driving her down onto the ground. Mud filled her mouth and covered her eyes. She threw her arms over her head to shield herself from the cement blocks and tree branches. Michael did the same. After about ten seconds the mud stopped falling.

Gasping for air, Buffy dug her way out. Beside her Michael's hand stuck up from the field of brown. She grabbed him and pulled as hard as she could. His head came up, his beautiful face covered in mud, just as her feet slipped out from under her.

Buffy landed on her back with a splat and lay there, the angel beside her.

CHAPTER SIXTEEN

Willow let her head drop down. She was exhausted. She'd poured every ounce of magickal power she possessed into the Belial siphon. She'd even taken power from Xander, something she hadn't wanted to do, ever. She'd opened herself to the dark forces within the magick, but she'd managed to hold on to her control over them. She'd faced her fear and triumphed over it.

But it was all for nothing.

The magick circle was still in place. The candles burned brightly. The brown-stained notebook lay on the ground, not levitating. *Well, why should that be any different?* she thought bitterly. She wasn't sure what she'd expected. Maybe a wolf to come trotting back into the room, or a sheep. Or for the notebook to pick itself up and float the way it was supposed to, obliterating the two times when it hadn't.

Or for the world to end, maybe, completely undone by the strongest spell known to mankind.

She hadn't expected *nothing*.

"Gnineppah gnihtyna t'nsi yhw?" Xander asked.

Willow's head snapped up. "Tahw?" she cried. She clapped her hand over her mouth. What had she just said?

"No gniog s'tahw?" Dawn asked, frightened.

Frantically Willow glanced around the room. Was this the end? Did the apocalypse end with them all speaking gibberish?

One of the candles went out. Then the next. And the next. "Yeh!" Xander said, pointing at them. A tear slid up Dawn's cheek into her eye.

Willow could hardly believe her eyes. Things were going backward! "Drawkcab gniog era sgniht!" she announced happily.

Giles, Dawn, and Xander just looked baffled. Didn't they get it? She was speaking backward! "Drawkcab gniklat m'I!" She giggled. "Gnikrow s'ti!"

Giles jumped up from the bed. "Gnikrow s'ti!" he agreed.

Sharp, pure joy rushed through Willow. It was working! Her magick had worked!

Buffy couldn't see anything. There were tiny black specks flying through the air all around her. Circling and buzzing . . .

Bees, she realized. Bees again? That didn't seem right. They encircled her, coming closer and closer. She squinted at the wall of insects. They were flying backward. Buffy whirled around, looking for Michael.

He stood behind her, staring at the ground. Buffy followed his gaze.

The bees were disappearing back into a broken clay bowl on the ground.

Michael looked at her, the question obvious in his blue eyes. But Buffy had no answers. What was going on?

The broken broom handle flew up from the floor, landing in Anya's hand. Startled, she glanced around. She was in the Magic Box, and it was a wreck.

Anya frowned. Hadn't she just left here? In fact, hadn't she bid the place a final farewell and good riddance?

She was sweeping, collecting dust, plaster, and broken glass into piles in the corner. She had to bend over practically double to use the stupid broom, but she was powerless to stop herself.

This completely sucked.

Spike crouched behind a dead bush, watching Buffy with Michael in the dining hall. Those blasted glowing corpses kept blocking his view of the Slayer, so he moved over to the next bush.

The so-called angel was in clear view now. Spike ducked, terrified in spite of himself. So much for watching Buffy's back. He scratched at one of the painful red itchy things on his skin. It became more painful, like a hot iron stabbing through him. In fact, all of the red welts were painful. It was almost more than he could take.

Then they vanished. Spike stared in amazement at his arm, back to its normal deathly pale self. He collapsed onto the ground in relief.

It was where the creek should be, but the water was frothing and foaming, a raging river. Buffy frowned down at it. It was familiar. . . .

Then she heard the hiss of the sea monster. She glanced up as its snakelike body slithered back down into the water. Its sharp teeth gleamed a foot from her face and she got one last whiff of the sushi breath before it slipped back under the water.

Buffy grinned. She was getting the hang of this now. Things were reversing themselves. Michael would be across the water in a second.

She looked toward the far side of the river, and sure enough, there he was, standing amidst a pile of her weaponry. Buffy jumped up and down, waving to him with what she could just tell was a big idiotic grin on her face. "Drawkcab gniog er'ew!" she yelled.

"I know!" he called happily.

Giles watched as the thick clouds rolled out of the sky, leaving the California sun beating down with full force. He sighed with pleasure. It was good to see the sun again. He had a feeling it had been gone for a while.

He'd taken full precautions, putting on sunblock and the like, but it was still certainly more sensible to be inside in such weather. Of course Buffy had insisted that they all camp out for the afternoon, pretending they were at the seashore. He didn't understand Americans and their obsession with sunshine.

Ah, well. He had his book. And it was good to see his Slayer acting like a normal girl for a few hours.

Besides, his interior meteorologist was telling him they were in for another change in the weather soon.

Dawn stood on the sidewalk near the house. For some reason she felt that she should be getting mad at Buffy in a minute. But for now all she could do was stare into the sky.

Giant, sharp-edged hailstones were flying thick and fast—from the ground back up into the sky.

Dawn watched them go, a slow smile spreading across her face.

The smell of eucalyptus filled the air, and Buffy heard the gentle splashing of the water in the fountain. She was in the park at night, near the angel statue—her favorite place. And there was a lamb caught in a thorny bush.

Buffy stared down at it, shocked at how tiny and cute it was. The lamb gazed back at her with big, sweet brown eyes. Then it stood and took a few steps backward, yanking its soft wool free of the bush. It began to trot away from her, backward. Somehow Buffy was able to run forward, chasing it.

The lamb picked up speed, racing through the park. Buffy sprinted, feeling the wind in her hair, the cool night air soothing her hot skin.

The lamb's fleece was changing now, becoming coarse. Becoming fur, not wool.

It was on the streets now, heading toward Buffy's house. She knew she didn't want to catch it. She just wanted to follow.

The lamb's hooves separated into toes and became paws. It grew taller, and thicker, and nastier. It became a wolf, and it spun in one quick move to face Buffy. It stood in the middle of the street in front of her house.

She stopped running and stared into its yellow eyes, mesmerized by it in spite of its snarling. "A wolf in sheep's clothing," she whispered.

The wolf vanished into a flash of white light, which shot through the air in the direction of her house and disappeared into Willow's bedroom window.

Buffy gazed at the window, a feeling of peace seeping through her. It was okay now. The wolf was gone. No, the sheep was gone. Wait. Had there been a sheep? Why would there be a sheep on her street?

Buffy glanced down at her hands. She was holding her cell phone. She looked back up at Willow's window. She was patrolling, wasn't she? Why was she back home already? She couldn't even remember how she got here.

"Huh," Buffy said, sticking the phone into her pocket. "Gotta lay off the crack."

CHAPTER SEVENTEEN

*Willow and Xander sat on the floor of the bedroom
in a magick circle made of white chalk. One by one she
lit the three candles between them as Xander placed a
thin notebook on the ground. Willow's hands shook.
She was nervous.*

"Now what?" Xander asked. "Join hands?"

"Not yet. You have to smear some of this on the
book," Willow said, handing him a small glass pot full
of a brown substance.

"Got it." Xander did as she asked, then put the
glass stopper back on the pot. He reached for Willow.

"Oh! Wipe your hands first," she said quickly.

He raised a questioning eyebrow, but obediently
wiped his fingers on his jeans. They joined hands.

"You're freezing," Xander said, concerned.

"I'm okay," she replied. She met his eye and smiled a little. "As long as you don't count the, you know, soul-deadening fear."

"There's nothing to be afraid of," Xander said. "It's just a little levitation spell. What could go wrong?"

"I could lose control, get addicted to the dark magicks again, and destroy the world," Willow suggested.

Xander squeezed her cold hands. "I didn't let that happen last time, and I won't let it happen now."

She smiled, touched.

"Remember, we're just easing back into the magicks," he said. "This one is so simple even a tenth-grade version of you could've done it. Even I could probably do it."

"Don't get all delusional on me," Willow teased. The nervousness was fading from her voice.

"You ready?" he asked.

She nodded uncertainly.

"Then tell me what to do, boss lady," he said.

"Concentrate on the notebook," she told him.

They were silent. A fly buzzed through the air around Xander's head. "I keep thinking about ice cream," he said.

"Hush," Willow reprimanded him. "It won't work if you don't concentrate. Close your eyes." He did.

Willow kept her eyes open for a moment, staring at her best friend, needing to fortify herself. Finally, swallowing her fear, she closed her eyes and began to speak. "In the world, we are blind. In the candlelight, we see."

Michael moved closer to them, although they

would never see him here even if they were looking. He placed a hand on Willow's head. She was so brave, and she didn't know it. She still had so much to do before the end.

Xander was trying hard to keep his eyes closed but Michael knew he wasn't really concentrating. The fly was bothering him. Michael caught it in his smooth white hand. "Elsewhere," he told it. The fly headed out the window. Michael placed his hand over Xander's head now. "Learn to focus," he murmured. It was a wish, not a command. "Buffy will need you. You're the engine behind them all."

Now he turned his attention to the notebook. The brownish smear on the cover was wrong. Michael could feel the wrongness radiating out of it. He placed his hand over the book. "Avaunt," he said. The brown smear disappeared. "Replenish," he said. Another brown smear appeared.

Michael relaxed, satisfied. The wrongness was gone, the danger removed.

"In the world, we lie still," Willow continued, her voice strong and clear. "In the circle, we fly!"

As he faded out of the room, the notebook lifted slowly from the ground, floating into the air as if made of helium.

Xander cracked an eye open. "Will, look!" he cried. "It worked!"

She looked, and smiled.

"Nothing bad happened," he said. "Didn't I tell you I wouldn't let the world end?"

• • •

Buffy checked the Day-Glo orange watch Dawn had given her after she'd come home late one too many times. She'd been patrolling for a few hours and had already hit most of the cemeteries. Maybe she'd call it a night. There was nothing happening in the park. Well, not unless you were looking for a quick hookup, which Buffy definitely wasn't.

And she wanted to get back home to Willow. *Not that Willow needs supervision,* she thought, feeling guilty. *Just a friend.*

The sensation of déjà vu tickled her brain. *I've thought that thought before,* she thought. Of course she had. Or something like it. Because she'd been worrying about Willow a lot.

I'll circle by the angel fountain, then jet, she decided. The clearing with the fountain was her favorite part of the park. The smell of the eucalyptus trees nearby always felt as if it actually got down into her lungs and scrubbed them clean. And if she'd had a really brutal patrol session, she sometimes kicked off her shoes and stuck her bare little piggies in the fountain's bubbling water. The eucalyptus and the bubbles were almost as good as a fancy spa. And the statue took her breath away. This angel was no fat little cherub. He was *manly.* As long as you ignored the long dress he wore.

She pulled out her cell and hit speed dial one as she headed over. Her own voice greeted her. She wished she didn't have to listen to the message. She thought she sounded like a six-year-old girl on the machine. Her voice wasn't really so high and squeaky, was it?

And she was déjà vu-ing again. *You think that thing about your voice every time you hear the message,* she reminded herself. But the feeling was so strong. It wasn't the same as—

"Hey, Will, you there?" Buffy said as soon as she heard the beep. "Dawn? Anybody? No? Okay. Willow, or Dawn, dinner thoughts? No food in the house, of course. So . . . menus. Still in the same kitchen drawer, Will. Probably exactly the same menus. Whoever gets home first does the dialing. And choosing. See ya."

Buffy clicked the phone off and jammed it into the pocket of her tailored leather jacket. The soft trickling of the angel fountain caught her attention, de-stressing her immediately. She slowed as she entered the clearing. Something was different tonight. The air around the fountain felt charged, electric.

She stepped closer to the angel statue, studying its marble face. It was beautiful. She'd never noticed before how beautiful he was. Buffy felt giddy with happiness suddenly, just from being in the vicinity of this gorgeous angel. She tilted her head to the side, gazing at the statue.

It reminded her of something . . . someone? "Michael," she whispered. But that didn't make sense. She didn't know anyone named Michael who was this beautiful.

But it didn't matter. Nothing could disturb her serenity right now. This place felt enchanted. A soft golden glow appeared in the trees, resolving itself into a globe of yellow light. It moved slowly through the eucalyptus, then floated toward Buffy, circling her slowly.

Buffy bathed in the warmth of the light. She had no idea what it was, only that it was there to protect her. The light had an almost physical presence. When it moved through her hair, it felt like a soft kiss on her forehead.

The light left Buffy and floated to the angel statue. It circled the angel lovingly, and then in one swift move it dove into the top of the angel's head and moved downward through the rest of the statue. For a moment the entire angel glowed as if lit from within. Its marble face seemed alive with light, and Buffy could swear it was smiling at her.

Then slowly the golden light faded. The angel's face went back to normal as if it had fallen asleep.

Buffy shook herself, her mind snapping back to reality as if she were waking from a dream. She turned to head home, feeling refreshed and hopeful. As she left the fountain behind, she smiled happily. "I love angels."

ABOUT THE AUTHORS

Laura J. Burns and **Melinda Metz** are obsessed with *Buffy the Vampire Slayer*. In fact, it was the chock-full-of-subtext writing on *Buffy* that inspired them to try writing for television. So far they have written two pilots and spent a season as staff writers on the late, great TV show *Roswell*. In the book world they created the Roswell High series written by Melinda and edited by Laura. Their next book is *Everwood: First Impressions*.

Everyone's got
his demons....

ANGEL™

If it takes an eternity,
he will make amends.

Original stories based
on the TV show
Created by Joss Whedon
& David Greenwalt

Available from Pocket Books
Published by Simon & Schuster

POCKET
BOOKS

2311-01

Buffy the Vampire Slayer can toss a one-liner more lethal than her right hook—without breaking a sweat. Now fans of Buffy's wicked wordplay won't want to miss this exhaustive collection of the funniest, most telling, and often poignant quotes from the Emmy-nominated television show.

"'Her abuse of the English language is such that I understand only every other sentence. . . .'" —Wesley Wyndham-Pryce (quoting Giles) on Buffy, "Bad Girls"

Categorized and complete with a color-photo insert, this notable quote compendium will have you eagerly enhancing your Buffy-speak.

"If I had the Slayer's power, I'd be punning right about now." —Buffy Summers, "Helpless"

Buffy
the vampire slayer ™

The Quotable Slayer
The last word on life, love, and lingo in the Buffy-verse!

Compiled by Micol Ostow and Steven Brezenoff

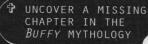